Dr. Bleak's Castle of Freaks

Dr. Bleak's Castle of Freaks

Karen Joan Kohoutek

Skull and Book Press

ISBN 978-1-7330307-0-0

Skull and Book Press, Fargo North Dakota

octoberzine.blogspot.com
octoberzine@gmail.com

Cover image courtesy of Historical and Cultural Society of Clay County.

Thanks to Mark Peihl for his archival assistance, and to Markus Krueger et al. for their work on the 2022-2023 Ralph's Corner Bar exhibit.

Author photo by Eric Wicklund.

For Madd Frank, and all the other horror hosts who keep us going.

"When we go but one step beyond the immediate sensible qualities of things, we go out of our depth."
— Edmund Burke, *A Philosophical Enquiry into the Origin of Our Ideas of the Sublime and Beautiful*

Night of *Night of the Living Dead*, the time slot just before Dr. Bleak came on the air at midnight. Zombies were on the loose, and it didn't look like the survivors were going to survive. Even if you hadn't seen it a million times, you could tell that if you'd ever seen a movie before in your life. As a ghoulish hand reached out to grab the biggest asshole in the cast, a frantic pounding started up at my door.

I jumped, as startled as if it had flung open and someone dead had grabbed at me in a burst of herky-jerky camera, all the more uncanny for the fuzziness of the TV reception.

Holding my hand over my heart attack, I got up off the floor and went to the teeny peephole in the center of the door. I could see a distorted face on the other side, one of the girls who lived down the hall, who I assumed just by the looks of them were El Ed majors—Elementary Education. What was her name again, like Monica?

I unlatched the chain, and when I opened the door, she almost fell in face first.

"I saw your light on," she said. "I'm sorry, I just didn't, I mean, I don't know."

She was aggressively normal, wearing a pastel yellow polo shirt with matching shorts. Her blonde hair, carefully icicled with paler streaks, was tormented into the ubiquitous French braid. To compare and contrast, second nature after my years of English courses, my hair was lank and dark, beginning to bristle into split ends around the collarbone. I wore a faded skirt and a floppy black wifebeater, with no bra, because it was way too hot for that kind of nonsense. The whole ensemble came from the same thrift store, the one I called the Little Old Ladies, where I'd never paid more than two dollars for anything, including a whole wool suit.

"What's the matter?" I asked, assuming it was a creepy guy lurking around the garbage cans again.

It was around barclose. From the fifth floor, I had a great view of the traffic picking up on the old Main Street. A while ago I'd heard a screaming argument in front of the strip mall liquor store, one of the signs of a Saturday night starting to wear down. She'd probably been at one of the Frat and Sore bars, getting shit-faced with her pastel friends, and then what?

"You're going to think I'm crazy." She was talking much louder than anyone ever did in the hushed hallway, especially at night, and she looked both slightly flushed and slightly pale. That didn't seem too strange, though. In the last few years of college I'd seen a lot of people drunk.

The girl unhooked her purse from around her shoulder and nervously started to dig around in it. She came up with a tangle of keys on what looked like glittery fishnet, full of feathery doo-dads and bits of plastic that were obviously meant to look like crystal.

"Can I come in?" she asked.

I shut the door and led her to the little island of kitchen: a longish counter that stuck from the wall, like a wooden Murphy bed, with a stool on each side. There was a typewriter on the counter, and stacks of paper, books and notebooks, nothing involved with the eating of food, since that wasn't really part of my lifestyle.

Let's Call Her Monica seemed to be getting her bearings, although it is possible that the sound of a zombie massacre in the background continued to be slightly unnerving.

"I saw a ghost in the laundry room," she said.

Whatever I'd been expecting, it certainly wasn't that. My immediate thought was "Cool!" but I didn't say it out loud.

Not that I believed her. But when she banged on my door I'd been sitting alone in the dark, watching a black and white zombie movie. A yellow-covered copy of Percy Shelley's *The Cenci* was sitting on my floor, next to my Penguin Edmund Burke and *Romanticism and Consciousness: Essays in Criticism*, bent so its spine and garish turquoise cover faced the ceiling. Literary-wise, I was primed to see a ghost. Besides, I'd take anything that would make this aesthetically hateful building more interesting.

"Let's go have a look," I said.

"No!" Monica cried, startled out of her fuss with the keys. "Are you crazy?"

"Okay, then. First thing. What were you doing in the laundry room?"

"I left my clothes in the dryer before I went out," she started, then added, "I know, I know," trying to ward off the lecture.

All year there'd been ongoing battles in the laundry room between invisible parties I had never seen, mostly in the form of hand-lettered signs. "Clean lint trap after every use!!" one screamed in especially bold letters. "Please be considerate of other peoples laundry!" was another, with a lack of apostrophe that had not been considerate of my nerves, grammatically sensitive as they were. It was a struggle, but I had successfully refrained from correcting it.

One of the main rules was that if people needed to use the dryer, and it was still full of leftovers, they were supposed to put the other person's laundry on the long counter built into the wall. But tenants kept finding their clothes lying in the puddles and streaks of water that seeped along the floor to the indented drain. The floor was cement, and it always had a layer of dark scum over it, so the clothes would not only get wet again, but would end up dirtier than they were to begin with.

More notes had been left, with, I assumed, old slights built into pretexts for laundry-related vengeance, which led to muffled arguments in the hallways, and accusations about parking spaces, which, luckily, I was too broke to be involved in. Since I couldn't afford the extra thirty bucks a month for the garage unit, I wasn't exactly affording a car to put in it. But after that whole brouhaha, there were three signs posted in the smallish room reading: "Do not use machines after 9 PM!"

"I just, I really wanted to get them done before I go home on Sunday. And I had to go out tonight. It's the end of the school year, so everyone was going to be at the bar."

"So you tempted fate," I said. "And you went into the laundry room." It was a dank cave at the best of times, so she must have been at least a little tougher than she looked.

"Well, yeah. The lock seemed weird, like a lot of the locks stick, but this one felt really sticky. Like it was resisting me. And then I got the door open, and I reached for the light, and I swear, someone was in the room. There was someone standing right next to me. I saw it just as I reached for the switch. I could have touched it. And when the light came on, it was gone."

"Did you get your laundry?"

A piercing scream suddenly emitted from the TV. Monica jumped. She was beginning to look totally sober.

"Fuck. I didn't."

"Let's go down. If the coast is clear, then at least you can get your clothes."

She looked at me like she'd never seen me before, although, to be honest, she hardly had.

"Really?"

"Sure." I mean, I had seen *Night of the Living Dead* before. I gathered up my own keys, slipped on a pair of olive green espadrilles with handwritten Anarchy signs all over them, and went toward the door, Maybe-Monica following me like a child. As we made our way to the elevator, which was kind of a creepy story itself, she suddenly said, "What if there's someone in the building?"

I hit the black push button. The elevator door slid open with a creaking sound.

"There's lots of people in the building."

"I mean someone who doesn't belong. Someone…"

"Lurking?"

"Well, why not? You hear about these things happening. The elevator groaned, shivered almost imperceptibly.

"And also invisible? You turned the light on, right? And there wasn't anything there." Listening to me talk, you'd have never guessed that she was the one preparing for a practical career.

"But maybe, I don't know. Maybe they hid."

Superstition was one thing, but actual life was another. It was almost always less scary to be afraid of something that didn't exist. Before the movie started, I was reading Edmund Burke, about the relationship between the sublime and the terrifying, and how darkness and vagueness were more sublime than light and clarity. But when the thing to be afraid of was actually real, then light and clarity only made that more clear and obvious, and Burke was pretty confident that for something to be sublime, it couldn't be anything that could actually hurt you in real life. That was a different kind of terror.

The elevator door slid open into a half-dark hallway, and we stepped out, reticent. Down there, the apartment doors looked particularly drab, and the windows always looked dirty from the outside. Some of the light bulbs were burnt out, as if the resident manager never came down, and maybe he didn't. The laundry room was at the end of the hall, with a window in the door, a pattern of wire mesh in the glass. I still had my keys in my hand, ready to open the door, but first I went up to the smeary rectangle and leaned my face into the glass.

"Can you see anything?" Monica whispered.

All I could see was darkness. There were no windows in the laundry room, and the dim light from the hallway only reflected my own face.

Brocken, I thought.

That was something I'd gotten from Coleridge and his ilk. They were really into the sublimity of mountain ranges, and how there were illusions on them, reflections, that seemed ghostly. As far away as I was from all that, I could still stumble across brocken-equivalents. "Modern Brocken," my mind raced: that would be a good name for a paper. Nice assonance.

"Nope." I put the key in the lock and started to turn it. Monica backed away instinctively. Whatever it did before, this time the lock didn't make the slightest catch of friction. It welcomed us right in. I realized that I was holding my breath with expectation, and I breathed out, impatient with myself. I looked left to right, reading the room book-wise, looking for subtext.

Nothing. How disappointing.

I switched the light on.

The bulb glared the room into a fluorescent pallor. Even that made Monica start slightly behind me. In that second, I would swear, will swear, that I saw a woman a few feet away. Just a normal-looking woman in a sundress. There was nothing distinct about her in any way, apart from being in a dark windowless room and then disappearing almost instantly.

"Did you see?" I trailed off.

"What?" Monica drew up next to me. We both looked in, crowded together like girl detectives gone awry in very different ways.

"Nothing."

The room couldn't have been more ordinary. The washer and

dryer, the counter along the wall, stuff leaning in the far corner—a mop handle, a broom handle. Monica's clothes lay in a heap under the counter, but they didn't look sodden. Her laundry basket sat quietly, peacefully, on top of a dryer, holding court, and she darted in to hastily gather up her clothes in it.

I quickly scanned around the room again, more critically, looking for anything that could be mistaken for a ghostly mirage. Nothing was really reflective, and the mop and broom were nowhere near the light switch. So as soon as she had her things, I grudgingly turned off the light and pulled the door shut, hard, listening for the decisive click of lock.

"Let's get out of here," Monica said, hugging her laundry basket.

On the way back upstairs, she said suddenly, "I thought it was that guy. You know. The one in the basement."

I knew who she meant. There was a guy who always stood in his basement window, looking out at the back steps, with the same blank expression, never reacting to anything. At that angle, his lumpy head looked like it was set up on a platter, the window frame cutting him off at the neck. I had never seen him in the hallway, only from outside, but from his placement, he must live down the hall from the laundry room. If I'd seen him in the dark, it would have freaked me out too.

We got off at our floor and Monica thanked me awkwardly. I shrugged it off, and we want into our separate apartments, her to get ready for her move back home and the job she almost certainly had at the mall, and me in time for Dr. Bleak.

3.

Thank god, or whoever, that the fake ghost hadn't kept me from seeing the beginning of Dr. Bleak. The monologue was the part I looked forward to the most. I hadn't even missed the ad for the Cornpopper's grocery chain, Dr. Bleak's main sponsor.

My apartment was like living in a spot where multiple closets converged. Besides the kitchen, there was a tiny bathless bathroom, the towel rack and shower frame all strung up with men's shirts from the thrift store, that I hand-washed in the sink. A partition, a little more than waist high and stacked with books, separated the bedless bedroom from the so-called living room, where I sat on an old floral sheet, spread out on the floor like a picnic blanket, a pillow leaned against the partition.

The screen went black. Around the edge, a frame sketched, white on black, and words formed, like the title card for a silent movie. Creaks emerged from the screen, like dungeon doors on rusted hinges, opening for the first time in a century.

"Welcome," an equally creaky voice intoned, "to *Dr. Bleak's Castle of Freaks.*" The camera began to pan around the interior of a dungeon, probably made of cardboard, where metal cuffs clamped surprisingly realistic skeletons to stone walls.

Almost perfectly simultaneously, sound began to throb through the floor. My neighbors were home from the bar. They always seemed to think they were the only people in the world with a record collection. An intermittent, continual jerk of music poured up, nothing in a rhythm I could get used to and easily ignore. I turned up the TV slightly. I was outgunned, but still, for their benefit, I hoped tonight's movie would have a lot of screaming.

"This is the world where the freaks reign supreme," the voice continued. "Here the taunts of the normals are turned against them, and the woman with a hand growing out of her forehead is the fairest of them all."

The camera turned to Dr. Bleak, sitting calm in an ornate upholstered chair, looking like a slightly wild-eyed clergyman. He wore a top hat and a formal suit, and at first glance he seemed perfectly normal. He wasn't painted like a ghoul, and his hair didn't bristle up like a mad scientist, two of the classic looks for horror movie hosts. The more he talked, though, the crazier he got, like a guy who might harangue us down at the Egyptian Bar.

"Tonight's film is set in a carnival, the carnival of freaks and mutant maniacs that some of you call the real world. In that world, there is nothing but cruelty and pain for the feeling soul. Only in the world where the mummies walk and the monsters howl their pain to the moon for the world to see, standing proud in their hairy flesh and their fangs, claws burning with innocent blood, and the blood running in the streets reflects the blood red of the sky, where the apocalypse is bursting forth, only there can love truly blossom. In this world, the pain is unbearable. In the other world, the pain is gone. Cross over with us, then, to the utopia of suffering, to the torture garden we call, *A School for Ghouls.*"

The credits started with a jazzy flair. Black and white, fifties or early sixties, a college campus with girls in turtlenecks and pointed bras. The title burned outward, in drippy letters, the cheesiest graphics ever. I loved it already. It was the kind of movie where the lead actress would be filmed through a haze of Vaseline, and conversations would cut back and forth between her, muffled and softened, and the hero, in clear focus. It would look like the two were talking through different time zones, one in twilight, the other in broad day.

"Boy, Professor Blutstein is sure piling on the homework," a blonde girl on the screen was saying.

"But he's so brilliant!" her obligatory brunette friend said. "He won the Transylvania Prize in Science three years in a row. The school was lucky to get him."

"I'm sure your dad knows what he's doing."

"It is a strain on him, being the headmaster."

They appeared to be surreptitiously glancing down at their scripts between sentences, their eyes darting down and then facing the camera to woodenly deliver their lines.

"If only he approved of Tom." The brunette pouted prettily.

"Don't worry, Marlene. Someday Tom will prove what kind of stuff he's made of."

I plumped the pillow onto the floor and lay down, curling to fit the shape of a non-existent sofa. I didn't know I fell asleep until my eyes jerked open. The students who were failing his class, or were just plain too disrespectful for Dr. Blutstein's European sensibilities, were getting turned into monsters in the boiler room under the girls' dormitory, vats boiling and fuming, but somehow inconspicuous. Rubber monsters, lower than the donation dumpster behind the Little Old Ladies.

As I dozed off, it felt like the actresses were walking over my grave.

4.

"I've never heard of this show," Vonn said the next night, at the Egyptian Bar. "What channel is it on?"

"Just the local station. Oh, and apparently my laundry room is haunted. Not that this is a surprise to me."

"What?" Vonn yelled over the jukebox, incredulous.

"But anyway. Dr. Bleak is the best horror host ever," I went on. "He's what Thomas De Quincey would be if he were alive today." She ignored it when I said things like that. That's why we were friends.

When I got there, she was already settled in with a bunch of her friends. "We got a pitcher!" she cried out when she saw me. I reached into the flurry and grabbed an upside-down glass, tipping it right-side up. The liquid sloshed into it, half a glass. She didn't care if I paid, but I didn't like feeling beholden.

It was pretty early. The opening band was still on at the Jigsaw across the street, so there were plenty of people in the Egyptian Bar, killing time. The long counter filled up on one end with the old-timers, guys who had been coming there for years. A few of them played pool, some who looked old, at least fifty, and some who were younger than that, with hippie hair and hard-living faces. We sometimes played pool in the back room of the Jigsaw, but not here, where people took it way too seriously.

Usually, the crowd got younger as the night drew on, until by closing there was nobody but college kids, except for the old guy behind the bar, who looked like he'd been back there for a hundred years and would outlive every one of us.

"Did you hear," Mike said, "that the Liquor Station is closing down?" He was one of Vonn's friends. Like most of them, I knew him from around, but I'm not sure I'd recognize him if he wasn't with his group.

Another one, a girl with one long tail of braid flipped over her right shoulder and aggressively geometrical earrings, was outraged. "You're shitting me," she said.

The Liquor Station was one of the yuppie bars, on the way to the highway, so you had to have a car to get to it, which told me right up front that it wasn't for my kind of people. It was a hang-out for El Ed kids and girls who went to the nearby private Jesus College, and had a reputation for being so full of assholes that a lot of people called it the Date Rape Station. Vonn and her friends sometimes went there anyway, like they did with the Dramarama Dance Club, if the specials were good, or if someone had a thing for a thick-necked poser boy they met at a party.

We all went to see bands, but I didn't fit in with Vonn's friends. They dressed like New Wavers, and would actually utter the phrase "New Waver" with a straight face. Only Vonn had the decency to look ashamed of it.

During the school year I mostly hung out with my best friend Gloria, and people from my classes, but they were all gone for the summer. Our activities overlapped with the New Wavers, at the Egyptian and the Jigsaw, and we all went to the University of Refugees. That was the state school, always there for you when you didn't know where else to go, or what to do with your life. Most of us kind of washed ashore there, which was actually lucky, like landing on a deserted island completely at random and finding a great library with a copy of Samuel Taylor Coleridge's Table Talk. Of course, some people claimed they went there on purpose, but they weren't the kind of people I trusted.

But anyway, it was only with the smaller pool of people in town that I suddenly became cool enough for Vonn to hang out with. She was okay, though. We weren't really friends, except at the corner where the corner bars were, and I was a Romantic, where she was a Modernist. But we were both English majors. If we were a street gang, then the Egyptian, home to generations of hippies, drop-outs, and liberal arts majors, would be our god-given territory.

Occasionally kids from the Jesus College turned up at the Egyptian Bar, either openly slumming or looking for students from the wrong side of the tracks, like Philosophy majors and Creative Writing seminarians, to flirt with. I bit my tongue and tried to avoid brawls, but I never made any promises.

"Some new people bought the Liquor Station, but it's not closing," Vonn said authoritatively. She prided herself on knowing everything on the scene. "The White Horse Tavern is closing."

"They're tearing it down," James put in. He'd gone to high school with Vonn, and I knew him from the Brit Lit survey courses. He still thought of himself as an American Lit guy, but if I had to call it, I'd say he seemed to be shaping up as a baby Wordsworthian.

"Not the White Whore," Mike said. "That's too bad. They had the cheapest booze ever, in the history of time."

"It was awful, though," the girl who'd been metaphorically shat upon added.

"I think the dirt was the only thing holding it up," someone else said.

I'd never even been to this bar and they were pissing me off. If they cared about cleanliness they shouldn't have been at the Egyptian.

"The White Horse is open on Sundays," Vonn pointed out.

"I didn't think anybody could be open on Sunday," James said. "Isn't there a law or something?"

"The White Horse had some kind of thing," she shrugged.

At the jukebox, Harry Belafonte had given way to the Strawberry Alarm Clock. Two kids standing there were taking forever to pick out their songs, and they kept reading off the titles, loudly, in the fakest English accents. It was getting really annoying.

"Are you going over to the Jigsaw?" someone asked then. "Along the Watchtower is playing."

"Are you kidding?" I asked. "When a band's named after a Bob Dylan song, there's nowhere to go but down."

"Tad's pretty cute," the girl said. "And so's their bass player."

"Just because they're cute doesn't mean they don't suck," I said.

Vonn barked with laughter, and James joined in. The girl looked a little insulted, but dropped it.

"We'll probably go over later, when the cover goes down," Vonn said.

The bar was beginning to fill up. The jukebox got louder. A friend of James' came over with a shot glass of tequila and plunked it into the pitcher, where it foamed and slowly sank to the bottom. A muscular guy in torn jeans and a black t-shirt, painted with homemade anarchy memorabilia, stumbled up to our table. He'd been pacing around earlier, back and forth from the bar to the back room.

"I wanna get fucked up tonight!" he announced.

Vonn raised her glass. "Good for you, man," she said.

"Nobody tells me what to do," he warned, his hand instinctively making the pistol-trigger-point gesture at her. "So I'm gonna get fucked up."

"Nobody's stopping you," James said.

Somebody bumped the table hard as they went past, and a few precious drops of tequila-laced liquid splashed out of one of the glasses.

"Hey, watch where you're going," I Wanna Get Fucked Up said, voice tight and pinched. He made a vague gesture as if he was going to grab someone, but came up with only air in his hand.

"Look, man, be cool," Vonn's friend said.

"Nobody tells me what to do!"

After yelling over the "Walking the Dog," the kids at the jukebox had gone back to their table. When the Grateful Dead came on, half the room burst into a groan, and somebody banged his drunken forehead on the counter.

"We need some punk rock on this jukebox!" Fucked-Up yelled, circling back to our table.

Vonn made cheerleader whoo-whoo sounds, her hands in the air.

"This bar would be nothing without us." He leaned toward Vonn, his one fan, with eyes darting around, unable to focus. "This town would be nothing! It would be dead if it wasn't for all we put into it."

"It's still dead," I said under my breath, to James.

"And yet the dead walk."

Suddenly the old punk and Vonn were talking quietly. Then he abruptly jutted away, disappearing toward the back room.

"Hey," Vonn leaned over, slightly hushed. She was lighting up a cigarette she'd just bummed off him. "He's got some coke."

"And?" I said.

"I haven't done any in ages." She looked seductively across the table at James. "Are you in?"

"Maybe. How much?"

Her other friend was already getting out her purse.

"Jesus." I said. "You guys get arrested, I don't know you."

"What's the matter with you?"

"That guy is clearly crazy."

"Don't be so judgmental," Vonn said. "He's just a colorful character."

"He's not going to be discreet. Anyone who walks up to total strangers and offers them drugs is asking to get arrested. You don't want to get involved in that."

"Just because you don't like the white stuff."

"No, I don't. And when you two are doing it you make me crazy. 'What'd he just say? What's he talking about?' You can't carry on a thread for two seconds."

"Come on, don't you want to get busted with us?" Vonn asked. "It'll be fun." She passed the cigarette across to me and I dragged on it, delicious.

"No, and I don't have any money for your bail. Remember that."

"So you're going to leave us in the hands of a criminal?" James asked. "Some friend you are."

"I need a glass of water," I said as I got up, trying to avoid Fucked-Up's perimeter. I wound my way toward the bar, where a guy with a shaved head and a tattooed neck stood on one side, filling three pitchers of beer with one hand. He snapped the tap shut, and then there was plunking and shoving, wet bills passing along, a toweling of the bar. Most of the stools were filled with kids now, their backs toward the bartender and each other, talking to people standing in the narrow corridor between the bar and the tables. On the far wall, the third strip of seating, were the booths. Those were prime real estate, although Vonn tended to prefer the tables. They were easier to get in and out of, and she always had a lot of mingling to do.

It took a while to get a word in edgewise at the bar.

"Just a water," I said. The bartender didn't sneer, like some of them did, but poured it readily, like it was a relief not to have to deal with anything. I swirled the glass, watching the ice cubes bump, and looked over the sea of people.

Okay, it was more of a lake. This would be a slow night during the school year. Even so, on a Friday or Saturday night it would slowly get busier until the narrow walkways choked with people, every chair filled up, the back room waxing and waning as people went back and forth to the Jigsaw. By barclose it would be a smoke-filled mass.

Already hunched in the booths were the coolest of the punk rock kids, their drinks and cigarette packs stretched out on the embossed gold surfaces, including a handful of guys who looked like vampires, and Handcuff Girl, who dressed all in bondage leather. Along with them were a few familiar people, who were older and dressed down a little, who still hung out. They had seniority. In the aisle, it was probably all the guys in all the bands that played at the Jigsaw. They all drank at the Egyptian, especially before the headliner.

Going to the opening bands, and paying for drinks at the Jigsaw, was for suckers. Paying the cover charge was for suckers. It's crazy that the Jigsaw actually stayed in business. Somebody had to pay the cover. But nobody I knew ever paid to get in if they could help it, or ever bought a drink there, unless it was an emergency, or a really exceptional deal on pitchers.

Instead we went to the Egyptian almost every night, and most of the time I didn't even like it. A lot of the people were assholes. They did nothing but talk shit, and think they were cool, when they were nothing but college kids hanging around an old working-class bar they'd largely driven the working class out of. Although it's not like I was cool either. I was a loser. The Egyptian Bar was a place for losers. It always had been. That's why we were there. We wouldn't be there if we had anywhere else to go.

5.

I lost my job the last week of school. You needed to be registered for classes and paying actual tuition to have a job on campus, which seemed backwards from the point of view of why I needed a job. I kept going to the campus job service, looking hopelessly at the index cards pinned on the Community Jobs board. Most of them ridiculously required "own car and insurance," which wasn't going to do me any good.

Lying awake, on the flat futon stretched on the floor, I stared into the darkness, thoughts burning through my head, mostly about money. I thought about my bank account, which was so low they'd close it if I took anything out. There was a stash of cash in my dresser drawer, dwindling, the rent coming around again before I knew it, the lights I had to leave on. Or could I live without lights? Maybe I could go to sleep when it got dark, like a farmer, and buy generic non-dairy creamer instead of milk. Maybe there was something I could pawn. My friend Kim talked about pawning stuff all the time. But that was like her VCR, or her boyfriend's amplifiers. I had a little double-cassette boom box, and that probably wasn't worth much.

Maybe I'd have to move. I didn't have a damage deposit, but it wasn't impossible that I could find some kind of terrible roommate situation, a windowless room somewhere with a bunch of stoners, and a shared bathroom. It would be filthy, with a litter box that no one ever cleaned, shit crusted all over the floor. I knew lots of people who lived like that. This place was cheap, but they got cheaper. There was always further down I could go.

The next morning, before it got too hot, I walked down to the state job service. Their office was a whole ordeal, especially when the form asked me to write down the kind of jobs I wanted. It was pretty presumptuous to think that what I wanted had any relevance whatsoever. All they had were jobs that I didn't qualify for, and also more or less sucked.

However, I had once used a postal meter, so the counselor put that down as a "skill."

After that, I walked down to the fading downtown mall, to the Space Age Pharmacy. There wasn't anything Space Age about it; it looked like any other drug store I'd ever seen. But that's what it said, in big red letters right when you went in the door. I figured I'd better buy a pair of pantyhose, in case I got lucky and they called me about one of the horrible jobs.

On the way home, I walked along the railroad tracks for a while. There was a whole neighborhood full of gravel, busted rock, old warehouses with glass windows smashed into spikes, the screens torn out, half hanging, net flopping. Where the wood was painted, it had long ago faded into the walls, but still clung, readable with a squint, in flourishes of advertising for long-dead businesses. Tramps had shed clothes as they went, the fabric half ground into the earth, moldering into dirty smudges. The path was just veering into a full-sized sidewalk when I heard a harsh blast. The ground rattled as a freight train charged by, dust flying all around it. The noise was like sparks flying, an underlying beat of chug and thud, a rhythmic clatter, random shrieks and squeals as the metal wheels struck the metal tracks, and almost made my teeth hurt. It sounded like a punk rock song. I liked it.

6.

"This is my lot; for either still I find
Some imperfection in the chosen theme,
Or see of absolute accomplishment
Much wanting, so much wanting, in my self."

7.

It felt weird that the first time I ever went to the White Horse Tavern was its last night. The building was old, with a horse silhouette in shocking white neon in front, and walls of square white blocks, some of them cracked slightly. It looked like if you leaned against it, one of the wedges would just pop through and you'd fall into the bar, elbow first. It was just my kind of run-down aesthetic, and I was sorry we'd ignored it until it was too late.

A crowd immediately overwhelmed us. Just inside the front door, a pair of windows were papered over, and the white tile interior was dimmed by years of smoke, barely budged by the fan that roared in the ceiling.

"There's a nice claustrophobic ambiance in here," I yelled at Vonn.

"Absolutely." She craned, trying to see over people. "I don't know if we can even get to the bar."

"I don't need anything," I said. I didn't have any cash anyway.

"Well, I need a drink," she said, trying to wedge us forward.

"We have to commemorate," James said. "Otherwise it's like it didn't even happen."

"Booze is your scrapbook?"

"Exactly!" Vonn said.

Like the Egyptian, the bar had one of those long mirrors behind the bottles, bouncing off an infinite funhouse of shining glass and colorful liquid. All around it, on the frames and the wall, were hundreds of photos, postcards, fliers, a whole history of the human race tacked up, ready to be torn down.

I thought everyone there would be older than us, and a lot of them were, but it was a whole assortment, and almost an alternate reality, because I didn't know anyone. That never happened at the Egyptian, where even the strangers had familiar faces. In glimpses of the crowd I saw older ladies in floral dresses, their husbands quiet beside them, holding old-fashioned cocktail glasses. I thought of the old-timers at the Egyptian, what it would be like for them to be driven out. Some people can go anywhere. They have cars and credit cards and families, so time and place and distance aren't obstacles. But when something's all you have, it can be taken away no matter how small and dirty and stupid it is.

Vonn eventually re-emerged with two bottle necks in between her fingers, splayed out towards me and James, and a third, stable and solid, in her other hand.

"Take them," she yelled, then added, "What is this music?"

"It's the Band," James told her.

"God, more hippies. No wonder they're closing down."

The beer was terrible, a bitter nettle sting on my tongue, but I chugged it gratefully. We were all sweating in there.

"Okay, we've done it," James said. "Can we go back to civilization?"

"Just let me go the bathroom first."

I went with her, and we had to wait in line. Women with bleached hair and tons of eye shadow helped each other stand up, so drunk they didn't think to just hold onto the wall. Most of them were shrieking with laughter, and I wondered how many of the people in the crowd, dancing on its grave, didn't really care about it any more than I did.

Vonn grimaced at me on her way out of the Ladies' Room. It was the size of a closet, with cracked tiles behind the toilet and something leaking onto the floor. When I flushed the toilet, the whole wall behind it seemed to pulse with dripping water.

"You're leaving?" a strange guy yelled at us on the way out. "The night's young. We're going the way of all flesh!"

"I don't think so," Vonn said.

Another guy, less disheveled, and better-looking, came up next to him, to catch Vonn before she swept out the door.

"There's a party at our frat house," he said. "After barclose. A pretty lady like you is always welcome." He glanced at me and James.

"And her entourage," I said.

"Absolutely." He rattled the details at her, leaning in close, intimate towards her face.

"Maybe," Vonn said over her shoulder.

Outside, some kids who looked like skateboarders were smashing beer bottles and stolen beer mugs on the asphalt by the dumpster.

"Classy," Vonn said, then, "What do you think? Frat party? Belly of the beast?"

"You know my answer," I scowled.

"Let's just go to the Egyptian," James said. "I have new appreciation."

In the material world, I thought, people tend to overestimate how long things will last. Stone seems so permanent, especially compared to human flesh, with skin you can see through. People thought the White Horse would be there forever. I tried to shake off the pensive. Life was hard enough.

"Jesus, watch your driving," Vonn barked at James as we jerked into the street. "If we kill someone, I don't think they'll let us buy any more alcohol."

Back to our usual spot, we dropped down easily in an open booth. It was made for us. We'd hit one of those quiet pockets, with a few people at a table, and a group sitting around the bar, in full bullshit mode.

"Well, that was depressing," James said.

"Exhausting," Vonn agreed. "Who wants a pitcher?"

"I can get it," I said, and they both handed me some bills.

At the bar, a contentious voice down the line of bar stools was holding forth like he was in a lecture hall.

"Do you see anybody in here with wings?" he said, his voice standing out. "No. You fucking do not see anybody in here with wings. I rest my case."

I tilted a little to get a look at him. He was youngish looking, with sharp, almost foxy features, and long cobwebby grey hair pulled back in a ponytail. An old-timer who looked like a farmer replied in a gruff, deep voice, something I couldn't make out.

"I'm just saying, I don't know any more now than I did. None of us do."

"We could if we wanted to," another guy put in. He was tall and biker-looking. They seemed like a strange bunch, but that wasn't unusual for the Egyptian. They probably normally came in on Sunday to watch "the game," whatever that was, so it was no surprise I didn't recognize them. "Maybe we just don't want to know more."

"Content with our lot in—life." The ponytail laughed. "Fuck that." He leaned back in his stool, a mug in his hand, shots lined up in front of him. I smelled something like pipe tobacco, the creamy, expensive kind. He scanned around the room, and I got a good look at him. His face was a lot younger than his hair. His drinking buddies looked over their shoulders to see what he was looking at, finding nothing interesting. The farmer leaned over, and this time I could hear him.

"The trick's in the exertion of the will. Once you have that, it's no harder to create one thing out of thin air than another."

"Are you kidding me? If I had any will to exert, would I be on this fucking bar stool?"

They all laughed, raucous.

"That's what I'm saying, man," the biker said. "You don't like your fucking bar stool, but you're content."

"Apathetic, maybe," the ponytail conceded. He downed a shot and then dug into his mug. "It could be worse, though. I mean, look at that girl. Fucking clueless."

He was looking right at me. All three of them were looking right at me. I was too shocked to react.

Then they turned back to conversation, huddled facing the grill, away from me.

I marched over to them.

"What the fuck did you say?" I demanded.

A clean-cut kid with Nordic blond hair turned to glare at me.

"What's your problem?" he asked. He was sitting next to a girl whose hair was piled and teased and braided into a froth on her head, who giggled at me with disdain.

"Where did that guy go?"

"What guy?" the girl asked, her voice as flat as her giggle.

"Darren's in the bathroom, but I don't think he said anything," the Viking said.

I stalked away to get my pitcher and the guy called out, "Maybe you should sell me some of what you're taking."

Fucking frat assholes.

8.

I got up early for a job interview at a hotel, and I even put my scraggle of hair back in braids, which I thought showed initiative, and a willingness to conform, temporarily, to the standards of society. My office outfits were all hideous hand-me-downs with bulging shoulder pads and floppy bows, but I didn't make the rules. I'd found the job in the newspaper: fifteen hours a week, minimum wage, no experience required, and I was hopeful, especially since it would cost me to get there on the bus.

It was on the other side of town, the building shaped vaguely like a giant tepee, with a swooping roof. I waited in a room for a good forty-five minutes past the time of the interview before a harried middle-aged woman came in and started barking at me about the job, and how college students were always unreliable. Then she said something about how they think they're better than everyone else.

I barely got a word in edgewise, and when she looked at the application, that my experience was working in offices at school, she practically guffawed. I wondered what on earth people thought they were going to get when they specifically asked for no experience. Besides, I didn't think that turning the switch on a vacuum cleaner would be beyond my capabilities, but I suspected that mentioning it would make me sound superior.

I left pissed off at the waste of clean clothes, and the dollar it cost to get there and back.

9.

In the back room at the Egyptian Bar, the side door, the door of discretion, opened right onto the main street. You didn't go past anyone who worked there, so that's where you went if anyone was underage, or wanted to smoke pot. Across from the door was the restroom of discretion, that preppy guys came out of rubbing under their noses, and a door facing the railroad tracks. When it was hot, like tonight, it was open, the screen door held by a flimsy hook and eye.

Louis Armstrong was singing, pool was shooting, and a tie-dye in the far-back corner rolled a joint on top of the linoleum table, his friends making noise around him.

"So I got my grades," Vonn said. "How about you? Any surprises?"

They'd come in the mail, on tissue-thin paper, in a little envelope, like a grandmotherly birthday card. A, A, A, A. I'd put it into a folder with the copies of my final papers. "Christabel as a

Finished Poem." "Wordsworth and Whitman: the Expansive Tradition." "Social Rebellion and the Sublime." Whatever.

I snorted a little. "No."

"I finagled a B in that Whitman class."

"That's because Dr. Brown loved you so much. You always wore those low-cut tops," James reminded her.

"Fuck you. God, you've been like this all night. I know you need to get laid, but there's no reason to be an asshole."

"Nobody in this bar," I said, "needs a reason to be an asshole."

She looked around the smoky room. "By the time we graduate we'll all be experts in the multiple asshole varieties. We can start an academic conference."

"Seriously," James said. "You're the one in a pissy mood, and that's why you're so down on everyone."

"Fuck you, you're drinking my beer."

She stood up, grabbed the pitcher and stalked away, clutching it to her chest, back into the main room.

"I paid for half of that fucking beer!" James yelled after her, dumbfounded.

"She'll be back."

"Yeah, but Jesus." He fumed a little, took a sip from his frothy cup, which he'd been lucky to refill just before she walked away. "I wonder if I should get another pitcher."

I leaned back and threw out my arms. "Your call."

We didn't say anything for a while. Vonn was the connection between us, and we usually just talked through her. The Ink Spots came up on the jukebox, like they usually did.

"I love this song," I said.

"Me too," he said. Then, "Do you know those guys back there, with the pot?"

"I think one's in Criminal Justice, but I wouldn't swear to it in a court of law."

"The one in the weird hippie sweater, like he wants to be a goat herder," he said. "He's with the literary magazine. That is everything wrong with the state of literature in this country today. Everyone is just a trendy wannabe."

"I don't think our generation could possibly produce anything as self-absorbed as Ulysses," I countered. "If that's any consolation."

"You have awfully violent literary opinions."

"You started it."

"But in general."

I sipped at my bit of beer. "That's why I try not to talk in class, unless the professor is really desperate."

Vonn came up behind us with a new pitcher full of amber brown beer.

"Stanley was up at the bar being a fucking asshole," she said, still on her rant. "I seem to remember that they used to be funny assholes, but now they're just everyday jerks."

She plunked the pitcher down and dumped herself into a chair. "Like, they all think it's a brand new discovery that I have tits. Oh my God!" She stared down at the front of her shirt, and grabbed them. "They just appeared there in the last five minutes! I'm so frightened!"

She pulled out a blue packet of Dunhills and dangled a cigarette in front of me.

"Come on. It's the good stuff. You know you wanna."

I snatched it right up. She struck a match with a flourish and lit them both up like she was doing a magic trick.

"Mmm, tasty."

"Nothing but the best for us."

"Everyone's talking about how that kid was found in the river," James said suddenly. "I think he washed up in the park, just north of here."

"Man, did you hear about that?" the dude with the pot interjected, like James hadn't brought it up. "Isn't that so fucking creepy?"

"Oh, yeah." Vonn sounded bored about that too.

Suddenly the guys at the other table wanted to talk to us.

"The guy's parents are going to sue the school," one of them said.

"No, they're not," Vonn said. "It was in the paper. They're all in an uproar, but they're not going to sue anybody. School isn't even in session."

"Summer school."

She rolled her eyes, but took the joint the guy leaned over with.

"I heard how guys keep being found dead in the river, in other towns. It might be a serial killer."

"Give me a break," I said. "There's nothing strange about a college student turning up in the river. There's this new invention called alcohol."

It started getting noisier in the front room, penetrating our sanctum, and suddenly a clump of Vonn's friends, all flushed and sweaty, burst in.

"That was intense," one of them said.

"The headliners are going to look like the fake jazz art-rock posers they are," Mike put in, grabbing an empty glass and helping himself to some beer. "Either everyone's going to leave, or just like sit around and stare at them."

"I was right up by the speakers, and it was so intense. The floor was vibrating, and my fillings were humming. And there were fifty of us all just thrashing."

"Are the headliners really going to suck?" I asked.

"Probably," James said.

"I thought you said they were really good."

"I said I heard they were really good. But then tonight a lot of people are saying they suck live."

"I'm going home," I said. "You guys have fun."

"You just want to go home and watch your precious Dr. Bleak," Vonn sneered.

"You're the one who said everyone here is an asshole."

10.

"And others hurried to and fro, and fed
Their funeral piles with fuel, and look'd up
With mad disquietude on the dull sky,
The pall of a past world."
— Lord Byron (George Gordon), "Darkness"

11.

I cut through the Cornpopper's parking lot and then to my block, down the long narrow length of sidewalk, the brown windowless wall of garage doors shadowing down on me. I walked to the front foyer, its boxy glass lobby lit up by the hanging bulb lights, frosted white and bigger than whole globes of the world. In the window of the basement apartment closest to the lobby, I could see the head of the creepy guy in the basement. As usual, he didn't react to my presence in any way.

It didn't seem like he was looking at anything particular, or maybe anything at all. He just stared out from a dark room, only visible because he was so close to the glass. I'd only ever seen him looking out the window in the back of the building before, at the same level, nothing below the neck. His apartment must have run the whole length of the building, a lot bigger than my little square of the world.

Up the steps, carpet threadbaring under foot, a metal door for every floor. The corridor of the fifth floor seemed slightly dim. The fixtures in the ceiling had square pieces of glass over multiple bulbs, and they would slowly dwindle away, a corner here, then another corner, until the square went dark. I hadn't heard anyone move into Monica's place, and the "Apartment For Rent" sign was still hammered into the grass outside, but that didn't prove anything.

The hallway was warm, too, but opening my own door felt like walking through a solid curtain of heat. I immediately switched on the big box fan, which roared to life, but its blade really didn't seem to stir up too much air. Then I flicked on the TV.

I tried to remember if I'd eaten. There was a pot of coffee that morning, and a slice of white toast. And yeah, that afternoon I stirred up some ramen for lunch. It tasted of salt and cheap soy sauce, and barely filled a cereal bowl, but I didn't notice during the day that I was hungry at all. I was getting out of the habit of eating. It must have been the little beer I'd had, priming the pump, reminding my stomach of its purpose. So I filled a coffee cup full of dry boxed macaroni to snack on, cracking them like nuts in my teeth, and sat down with Keats' letters, to flip through during the commercials, if I didn't fall asleep.

Sometimes, in the semi-dark, the opening creaks of Dr. Bleak seemed particularly unsettling. Which was definitely my money's worth.

"The cold shadow falls over the earth, and it's nighttime again. When it's hot, you long for the cold. Everything looks different. You see eyes in the trees; random shapes form into faces. So much is uncertain: the hand falls. The bone dries. The wall crumbles. Fear connects you to things. It makes you feel stronger to know that you're worth killing."

The film was called Cremation Ground. It seemed rough and grainy, a faint hiss behind it, like a videotape with bad tracking. It started with some kind of temple, in the middle of an overgrown forest, and an old woman, her hair full of ash. Smoke filled the background of the scene. It was another movie where the voices were dubbed and awkward, the way my own voice sounded so often when it came out of my throat.

Hidden in the temple was a scroll containing some ancient poems, and the old woman, who looked like a beggar, was the ghost of the poet, protecting the pretty heroine from other, malevolent spirits.

"Life and death are both mysterious things," the old woman cackled on the TV. "They go together like ravens and eyeballs. And everyone wants answers."

"I don't believe in spirits," the heroine insisted.

That made the old woman laugh more, stereotypically sinister, and it made me giggle along with her. "Does your existence depend on whether I know you exist?"

A body, wrapped in canvas, was perched on a pyre behind them.

"The living meet the dead halfway. The dead meet the living halfway," the old woman said. "That's the way things must be, for the balance between the worlds."

I suppose, because I was about her age, I should have put myself in the place of the heroine, but really, I could only picture myself as the old woman, with her crazy hair and bulging eyes, roaming the smoking wasteland outside the temple. An amazing score kept running on a kind of loop, a self-consciously spooky, sub-theremin sound, just enough to almost drive me crazy, but not quite.

After a commercial, the heroine couldn't convince the hero that demons were after her.

"That's nothing but old superstition," he said. "Nobody has a castle anymore. No one inherits a curse."

"But maybe you can!" she cried.

Maybe you could.

The heroine ran through the jungle, stumbling over bones, endlessly. It almost seemed that her spirit was trapped in the film, going in circles, startled by the same rubber snakes. If there was a god and a hell, that would be pretty bad.

Dr. Bleak said it all. "Because we used to be alive, doesn't make us experts on the living. And the living are certainly no experts on the dead."

12.

I found an index card on the bulletin board for a law office downtown. They wanted someone to make photocopies, with occasional mail sorting, and after all, I had that postal meter under my belt. It was designed for a college student to do, lasting only until school started, so I wouldn't have that black mark against me, either.

There was no way I could walk in this heat and look anything but bedraggled, so I dug out an old leather handbag with a really uncomfortable strap, big enough to carry a change of clothes. I tucked in my dress and my dressy shoes, which were flat and tan, with a hard bow glued over the toe tops. They were the color of that hideous foundation makeup people always tried to put on you at makeovers, like putty. I had never seen such ugly things in my life.

I walked in a loose tank top and a loose pleated skirt, with a pattern of tulips almost faded off; frayed, but nicer looking than the ugly polyester thing I had to change into.

On the last block before you crossed the river, the Egyptian Bar and the Jigsaw weighed down the corners, and they looked shabby in the dry dirty sunshine. Between the Jigsaw and the river was a dark chasm of auto parts store, full of mysterious chunks of metal and machinery. It looked virtually unchanged since black and white photos of the railroad boom, when the street was lined with old-fashioned groceries and department stores, pulled out by the roots a decade ago. On the other side of the Egyptian was a slope downhill to a small road weaving under the underpass. Just past that was a narrow stretch of drying grass and then the murky gray water.

Across the bridge, it was a different town, in another state, so when you walked across, less than a city block, you suddenly found yourself with a different drinking age. Maybe that's why the neighboring town was considered a little rougher in comparison, because they sent all their annoying teenagers to the Dramarama and the Liquor Station, leaving their own bars free for grown-ups.

The bridge's curved sidewalk ribboned along the road, separated from the cars by a low concrete wall and a line of metal framework, punctuated here and there by metal spikes. Garbage blew into the walkway, mostly cigarette packs, fast food wrappers, and a single clear plastic packet exposing a red condom, the color of a translucent candy.

Below, the river looked very far away, so prosaic and gray, drying into a trickle. The sloping sides of the riverbank were exposed, whole stretches of ground. It looked like mud had been spread over the earth, laid out purposefully, but it was just the river drawing back into itself, leaving part of its bottom behind. Tangles of dry tree branches reached up and bristled at the bottom of the bridge, and when I reached the bank on the other side, some of them were high enough to scratch at me.

The sidewalk sprouted into a long curve, alongside a busy, traffic-filled street, and I followed it past a big cement wall, to an underpass, that emerged surrounded by a sprawling complex of manufacturing on both sides of the street.

After that, I found myself on what passed for Skid Row. Brick warehouses and old movie theaters, plastered over with cheap storefronts, spread around two very large bars, one with a giant neon steer ripe for the slaughter, the other a giant, malevolent leprechaun. Doorways scattered with Lysol bottles had hand-lettered signs taped on them, offering rooms for rent, weekly and nightly rates, and there were a couple of pawn shops, their signs crying out about guns and more guns, reminding me that I couldn't afford to enter the Skid Row economy.

It wasn't so hot yet, still early, but the sun was already starting a glare. Once I was clearly going lengthwise down the street, it was suddenly a gauntlet of bums. They were all old, unshaven, calling after me and asking for change, the irony of which would have been funny if I hadn't been so outnumbered. It would have been worse in my interview outfit, but still, nothing good ever came of my wearing a skirt. The nylons screamed that I was a girl, which could only lead to trouble. One guy with a dirty beard shouted at me, something to do with his cock, but I didn't need the details.

Once I hit the city bus station, it was behind me, and I ducked in to change. A very large woman, wearing a heavy winter coat, stood moaning in front of the sink, her hands motionless under the faucets, no water coming out. She rocked her head back and forth, her body seeming to shudder. I went into the handicapped stall and stripped off my sweaty clothes, dabbed myself with toilet paper, and rubbed the spaces on my chest and back, where moisture had settled.

I struggled into the pantyhose. They were thin and spongy, and felt like they didn't let in any air. Underneath them, my legs had a sickly tint, not quite as far gone as orange. Then I put the dress on, wedging my other clothes back in the handbag. My shoulder already had a deep red gouge in it from the strap.

When I went back out and ran some cool water, the woman ignored me, moaning even louder, so I ignored her too. I palmed a dab of cool water over my cheeks and my neck, just a little, and rubbed it off with a paper towel. Then I brushed my hair. Semi-respectable. After a double check that there was no tissue sticking to me, and I was ready for a stroll down the block and around the corner, like a normal person who was prepared for a normal job.

The law office's building looked like it belonged in a more elegant town. The bricks were dark red, and looked freshly buffed. I rode up to the third floor in a fancy elevator, copper-colored metal elaborately carved. The controls were set in metal curlicues, and even the ding of arrival was hushed. I walked confidently to a reception desk and told the woman that I had an appointment.

"Michael will be right out," she smiled, warm. She had a bow on her blouse that looked a lot like the one on my tacky shoes.

Michael came out of an office and shook my hand heartily. He was tall and stoutly built, and of course he was wearing a suit. He looked like he'd never worn anything but a suit in his life.

"Let me give you the grand tour!"

As we strolled around the office, he gave me various brief, disconnected factoids about the business. None of the rooms looked very big, but there were a lot of them, connecting at odd angles. The break room counter held a very fat Mr. Coffee, baskets full of apples and oranges, and a plate of bagels: food that was just sitting there. Then we toured the photocopy room, which, if I got the job, would be my domain. Two high-speed photocopiers, and a wall of pigeonholes, large ones nearest the counter, shrinking as they got higher. On the counter was a postal meter, and wire baskets labeled with cards that read "incoming," "outgoing," and "to be sorted."

"Of course, we don't want anything to stay in 'to be sorted' longer than a few hours," he said.

"Of course," I agreed.

We ended up in his office. I sat on a bulging leather chair, facing him. Glancing down at my paper application, he asked a few questions about my previous job, and he clearly like the sound of it.

"Why do you want to come to work for us?" he asked.

That threw me off. These interviews weren't anything like getting a job on campus. I wanted to come to work for them because I had barely eaten anything the day before. I needed some money in the bank to pay the next month's rent, or my books and I would be thrown in the street. What was he talking about, and why?

"Well, I think it would be a great experience," I said. "The jobs I've had on campus have been a great starting point, but I'm ready to gain experience in a more ..." I paused. Don't say "grown-up," I thought. He'll think you're not grown-up if you do. "I guess a more sophisticated work environment."

He made a sound like a muffled chuckle.

"A job in the real world."

Sure.

"Exactly."

"Good. Now." His tone was maddeningly casual. "Where do you see yourself in ten years?"

Instinctively, I tried to visualize, and pictured nothing. A blank abyss. A sheet of darkness. An eternal black starless night.

Ten years? I had never even thought of thinking ten years ahead.

Well, he had my application in front of him, and he'd been reading it. That already told him what I was studying, so maybe I should have some plans for that. It seemed to be what people generally expected.

"Well, as you can see," I gestured slightly toward the paper in front of him, "I'm an English major. In ten years, I should have my Ph. D, and be teaching college English."

I could tell immediately that this was the wrong answer. A minute ago, he'd been ready to welcome me to the family, but his face had noticeably deflated.

"That's very ambitious."

"Well, I have a really good memory, and I'm a hard worker, so I think I can do it in ten years." Not exactly subtle, but it could have been worse. They always said you were supposed to sell yourself, and I thought my tone of voice was upbeat, absolutely nothing wrong.

"Well, thanks very much for coming in today," he said, and he had to glance down to remember my name.

He stood up to show me out, and I popped up too. I caught a glimpse then of the copper plaque on his dark oak door. "Michael Burke," it read.

"Huh!" I made an audible sound of surprise, and he turned to look at me, curious.

"Your last name is Burke."

"All my life," he said, a little of his jokiness back.

What the heck, I didn't get the job. "I've just finished reading Edmund Burke's book on the sublime and the beautiful," I said.

That made him seem slightly flustered.

"It's excellent," I went on. "There's a whole thing about the difference between horror and terror."

I reached out my hand, shook his firmly, and thanked him for his time. I went back out into the heat, growing even hotter, back to the bus station bathroom to change my clothes again. At least the woman wasn't rocking in front of the sink anymore.

13.

The Egyptian Bar by day: a dark sanctuary of artificial shadow, lit up in the artificial night by the beer signs behind the bar. Outside the sun beat down, the dead metaphor seeming literal, beating down, pummeling the street, punishing the earth for its existence. The stereotype of a sunny day is bright and happy, but this sun was pitiless, exposing the cracking sidewalks, the shabby cement, the crumbling walls and falling fences, shrubs and weeds dried to stick and wire. People weren't allowed to water their lawns or use their sprinklers, so everywhere the grass was crisping, the tips of every blade crinkling into yellow.

Even the air itself was dirty, the wind scouring the flat earth. Dust dirtied the blue sky. All of reality needed washing.

But inside, it was darkish, and even noticeably cool. The long bar faced a vista from which reality was excluded. The view threw yourself back in your face, in a foreground, where everything behind you seemed like it was in front of you. Behind the bar, a guy with a head shaved down to bristly-looking velvet leaned against the back counter, smoking. A couple of old guys sat in front of him, who seemed to have been arguing for a decade. "You tell him," one of them insisted gruffly to the bartender. "You get some sense into him."

"That's a big job," the bartender drawled.

"He ain't gonna listen to me."

In a few dark corners, other students sat with books and notebooks in front of them, jabbing their cigarettes in emphasis at each other.

I ordered a wine cooler, took a long sip, and leaned back in a dark booth, stretching my arms out on either side like I was putting them on the shoulders of an invisible friend. I stared at the gold table, the fine pattern traced on the surface, an ashtray emptied but unwashed, powder scattered around its rim, grey charcoal stains in its core.

Where did I see myself in ten years?

I didn't see myself anywhere, doing anything. I barely imagined myself existing in ten years. I wasn't entirely sure I existed right now. I tried to force my image, superimposed over some kind of life, wearing a pastel blazer and matching skirt, sitting at a desk in a cool place like that law office, where they made money doing inexplicable things. Who would I need to be, to have that kind of future? Not that I wanted it, but even if I did. Could I choose that, or was it something you just had, just were?

I leaned forward, ran my hands through my hair. Somehow I was doing everything wrong. Could I really choose to be a college professor? Right now that seemed as far away as becoming some kind of what: businesswoman? Just the thought. Me with business cards. Freelance literary critic. Ask for our low, low rates on poetry analysis. But there were kids in my classes that seemed destined for the classroom. They had something I didn't, too, as much as the lawyer did.

Maybe the difference between us is that they can see themselves doing something in ten years, I thought. It felt like I'd been given some kind of a key, even if it wasn't particularly helpful. At least it might explain a few things. Maybe some people had the ability to look into the future and think, what do I want to do? And they said, hey, I'm good at English! I'll be a teacher!

Come to think of it, that kind of made sense. I was startled to realize I had never thought of my life in those terms. It seemed so bald and mercenary.

Jesus Christ. Could I scrounge enough cash for another wine cooler? I didn't want to go home and sit in my apartment in this mood, and anyway, it was getting harder and harder to be there with nothing but my bad fan. The faint gray fragrance wafting from the ashtray, the smell of burgers in the boiling grill, lulled me. I never wanted to leave this booth.

Fortunately, I didn't have to, for now anyway. I dug through my awkward leather bag, brushing past the sad, limp flops of nylons and polyester, and pulled out the thin volume of *Nightmare Abbey*. At first it'd seemed too dark to read, especially when I first came in from the hot outdoors, but my eyes had imperceptibly adjusted, and now I had no trouble seeing the page.

Thomas Love Peacock. Now that's a great name for an author.

When I opened to chapter one, the facing page told me that this copy was published the year I was born. It was in pretty crisp shape, considering. Better shape than I was. I started to read, introduced to the satirical characters in their Gothic manor, "in a highly picturesque state of semi-dilapidation," a phrase that rose my spirits within the first sentence.

It was nothing like a Gothic castle in any way, but the Egyptian Bar was also in a picturesque state of semi-dilapidation, which was in my mind preferable to the more contemporary dilapidation I saw all over, like my apartment building, or the bus station. They weren't picturesque, just sad and wasteful.

"You know, I've never seen a cop in here," I overheard someone say.

"Having the cops come is like holding a séance. They've gotta be summoned."

The television set buzzed low in the background. A few old guys wandered back to play pool, bickering, friendly, over the pool sticks, and whether so and so had doctored them, whether they wanted to play with someone who always cheated. A kid stood by the orange-lit jukebox, completely unable to pick anything. In the book, the hero, Scythrop, went to college, where "his fellow-students… who drove tandem and random in great perfection, and were connoisseurs in good inns, had taught him to drink deep ere he departed."

Getting on two hundred years, and school was exactly the same. Only now I got to participate in the driving in tandem and random, and the drinking deep, which was the obvious improvement over time, despite all the aesthetic entropy that had gone on since then.

People came and went. Flares of little arguments broke up occasionally in the bar. The bartender stopped bothering to come around the booths, figuring if people wanted anything, they knew where to find him. I sipped at the wine cooler, making it last as long as possible.

14.

Some mornings I walked down to the library and read the paper with the other bums, all of us looking for work, or pretending to look for work, or just killing time. Some days I was only pretending, because it was perfectly obvious that there were no jobs for me.

A hell wind pushed people along the sidewalk. Grit blew hot into my face. I wore a pair of men's boxer shorts I got at the Little Old Ladies, dark blue paisley, with an equally cheap red bandana top, and a loose baggy shirt over that that looked homemade. It was nice not to have a job interview and need to pretend I cared what I looked like.

The library was so air-conditioned it was almost painful. When it got too cold, I'd sit outside for a little while under the trees, the heat sucking at me, and watch the cars go by. Guys huddled around the entrance, smoking, and threw their butts all over the sidewalk, in the grass. Some of them had bottles in their pockets that they pulled out when they thought nobody was looking.

The public library didn't have a lot for someone like me to check out, but I liked the atmosphere. I'd wander around, looking for old, peculiar titles, things they'd forgotten they had. That was the whole point of even going there. When I found anything interesting, I'd sit in one of the study desks, tucked inside its low wooden walls, with that rarest of things, free privacy.

In the stacks, I passed an old guy pacing against the back wall.

He wore a blue work shirt and gray pants, all slightly dirty. We politely ignored each other. But then, when I was leaving, I passed him again in the lobby.

"They're everywhere now," he lectured the empty air, gesturing at it. "And they're poisoning the living, Just like shit poisons the bloodstream." Some people coming in pretended they didn't see him, so I did too.

15.

"You turn on the TV, and there is a strange-looking man in a small room, talking to himself," Dr. Bleak said, peering straight out at me. "You are also a strange-looking person in a small room; an empty, midnight world outside. In your room with the single light bulb, night painted on the walls, listening to the figure on your lit-up screen, life is suddenly enlivened with death.

"You identify with his fantastical world. You think to yourself, wouldn't it be wonderful if people like this existed, if the grocery store at night was haunted by fiction, by drama or myth, something more than the lonely shabby people, struggling and shopping?

"He is your own patron ghost, the Ghoul that isn't in the Tarot deck, but should be. And while you're watching him, he keeps watching you, while you watch … *Carrion*."

The film's title card called it *Delirious Crypt of Doom*. It didn't match the rest of the opening credits, but looked like it had been dropped in randomly.

Discordant music blared over a dark screen. A nervous-looking man appeared in a slightly cockeyed close-up, looking over his shoulder. Then he screamed, for no apparent reason. Something dark swooped down, and blocked the camera, which shook a little. Then he was lying flat on his back, his face exaggerated in shock, Technicolor blood splattered all over him, oozing out of his mouth and framing his head.

Then there was—finally—an establishing shot of a graveyard: bare trees, the sound of wind blowing mournful and generic, a stone mausoleum amid tilted tombstones. Suddenly the camera hovered on a girl's back, pointed into the white cloth of her dress. The camera tried to follow her, but it seemed easily distracted. Then she screamed too, shrill and piercing. She jerked back and flung herself against the doorway of the mausoleum, her arms flung out, elbows bent, like she was in a silent movie. A knife appeared from nowhere, in extreme close-up, but she thrashed and ran.

It went on like that, completely disjointed, for close to an hour and a half. Images piled on each other, alternating between the tilted camera and the obtrusive close-up. Occasionally a character said something cryptic, and a second later the screen was full of bats, fluttering against a day sky, then a night sky, not matching at all.

"Something strange is going on," the heroine deadpanned, her mouth out of sync, as she stepped over an outstretched human hand, not even noticing it.

After the commercials, one for the local gas chain, which my friend Gloria and I called the Shop and Pay, Dr. Bleak popped in for a second brief monologue. "She's right," he said. "Something strange is indeed going on. You never know what will come out of the chimney … or the cellar … or the grave."

In the finale, an earthquake caused the tombs to cough up their remains, and the killer was attacked by a cloud of something, a cross between bats and locusts. The heroine looked on smugly, just watching. She and a cop, who I couldn't say was in the movie before, stood over the body, now draped in a bloody sheet, and made banal chit-chit.

"I'm not that young," she said, flirtatious.

The camera panned away, catching the hand of someone off-screen, on the ground, which was grabbing the forgotten butcher knife. The music made a dramatic, wavy sound.

"The End!" it cried, in a spiral of letters. They turned as if on a hypnotic wheel, and the words fell apart into a confetti alphabet.

Before he left, Dr. Bleak asked, "When did we start thinking that things had to make sense to be real?" As always, he made a lot of sense.

16.

For some reason I'd avoided the temp agency, but I had to give up. As usual, I felt clumsy in the cluster of calm women, wearing streamlined suits in the clean, airy room, surrounded by flower arrangements in tasteful blue vases. They didn't think there'd be much for me either, but maybe "light industrial," which they cheerfully synonymed as "blue jean work," obviously crap jobs where nobody cared what you looked like. My too-heavy corduroy skirt wasn't fooling anybody.

By afternoon, the light had the peculiar quality you get looking through dirt: see-through, but with a tinge, like a dirty lens. The world outside needed a fan, to stir up some air for my fan to catch.

I was lucky to get a few days of work from them. I helped with a survey, standing in the middle of the mall offering forms to people, and when anyone filled out the slip to win a free prize, I marked on a check box whether they were male or female. That gave me a little bit of money, minus the cost of the lengthy bus ride out there and back. At least it was air-conditioned.

The annoying thing about the temp agency was that I always needed to have clean clothes ready, in case I got called in. And then, the phone was an expensive conundrum. I didn't even want it, but it was the only way I'd know if the temp agency had something for me, so I had to keep it.

Every once in a while, I noticed that I could feel the bones inside my arms, rubbing against the surface. Or my elbow, the gears in my wrists. I could almost hear them squeaking. Then I'd think about times I'd blithely spent five dollars on some band at the Jigsaw I didn't even like, and then bought one of their over-priced drinks. What had I been thinking?

17.

Speaking of. Eventually I felt driven to spend a few dollars because I'd saved them up. But it was a band I liked, so at least it wasn't a pointless gamble of waste.

When Vonn and I got to the Egyptian and sat up at the bar, we faced an enormous sign that they were now selling jerseys and sweatshirts. One of them hung on the wall, floppy sleeves waving at us.

"Oh my God," I said. "That's all these people need to become more insufferable. Anyone with a pathetic desire to belong somewhere should be at the Liquor Station where they belong."

"Hey," the bartender came up to get our order. "You see we've got shirts in? Only ten bucks for the jerseys."

"I think not," I said, primly. Vonn got a vodka, and I got a water, and we swiveled to look at the makings of the evening.

"There's really getting to be a lot of tie-dyes here," Vonn said. Then she grinned, "You know that James is going to buy one of those shirts."

"Of course he is."

"After that, it's only a matter of time until he discovers the Grateful Dead, and hangs a paisley sheet in his window. And that'll be the end of hanging out with me."

I was laughing when James came up to join us.

"Do you have any change for the jukebox?" Vonn asked him.

"Someone's already up there," he said. "They won't play for forever, and we're going across the street."

"Not for ages," she sulked.

A friend of theirs, who I'd always called Che Guevara Guy because of his t-shirt with the famous silkscreen, stopped by with a couple of vaguely frat-looking dudes. Today he was wearing a Doors t-shirt. If he'd done that more often, I might have called him Jim Morrison Guy, but then, that was probably a fine distinction.

"We're going to Central America," he announced. "We're going to become revolutionaries."

"Do you have a particular country in mind?" I asked.

They were clearly stoned, so it was a struggle to explain their plan.

"That's amazing," James put in. "I can't wait until I can get out of here. I mean, I love the people here, they're great. But the Midwest is so petty and narrow-minded."

"But isn't it the people who make it petty?" I asked.

He glared at me. "You know what I mean."

"Not really. The geography, the weather, they don't make it narrow-minded."

He frowned and gave all his attention to Che Guevara. The more they talked about revolution, the more bourgeois they seemed. Before long it had all spiraled into politics, and we were all talking at once.

"It's no use trying to placate the conservative element, because you can't win," I heard myself say. "They don't think they have to justify anything, because they're normal."

"That's why this bar is so awesome," James said. He already sounded drunk, and we hadn't even gone across the street. "It's like a little community."

"You can buy a sweatshirt," I said, my voice sweet.

Finally we decided to go over, Vonn gathering up her bag. Outside, the Egyptian's neon sign poured light over the dark sidewalk, and the Jigsaw flashed across the street. The stream of headlights in both directions between them threw yellow onto the black asphalt, and the traffic lights sputtered their light into the melee.

Cars honked as they went by. Girls ran down the sidewalks, with a sharp hollow echo of high spike heels, a persistent clatter. Right in front of the door, a crabby girl was trying to push a yuppie into a parked car.

"Just get-in-the-car," she snapped.

"I think I'm going to throw up," the guy mumbled.

"Go ahead, it's your car," she said. "Do you think you can explain where you live?"

We went to the Jigsaw's side entrance, where it was easier to sneak in than from the more visible front. All it took was for the door kid to get distracted, called away for a second, which would happen, and then you could always pretend you didn't see the little hand-lettered sign with the cover charge written on it. Once Vonn knocked it down, and when the door kid came back before we slipped in, she found it on the floor. He ended up asking her out, but as usual, he was a drummer, so it didn't get past the first date.

A punk girl stood leaning against the industrial brick. She was pretty and pallid, and her waxen face was beginning to melt around her mouth and eyes. Her hair was tangerine orange, but inside, at the seam, it was the color of her leather jacket. She looked like she'd never had a full night's sleep in her life. As we passed her, a guy walked toward her, and before he could say anything, she shrieked "Fuck off!"

We waded through a swamp of beer, cigarette butts floating and tangled on the surface like weeds and algae.

"God, they haven't even sound checked," Vonn griped. "I swear to God, there's no point in having more than a couple of bands. It just devolves into endless rounds of plugging and unplugging."

"The first band has played, though, right?" I said. They were local, and we all hated them. We asked around in the crowd and got the answer we were hoping for.

"Now, their instrument really is the electrical socket," I said. "Working the power strip is the highlight of the show."

"Way better than their guitar playing."

James was talking to a girl with short black hair, all sharp and sculpted, except for some pieces sprouting out in back, too many of them to be tails. She took out a lipstick and held it like a cigarette.

"I know her," Che Guevara Guy told us. "I could fuck her any time I want to."

"Well, that's good to know," I said.

His frat brother rambled at us about bands that he liked, and I dismissed them all as fake punk.

"What's fake about them?" he asked, defensive.

"Because they're not really angry. It's just useful to them."

He shook his head. "You're awfully negative."

"Don't listen to me," I brushed him off. "I don't know anything. Well, I do, I know a lot of things, but nothing useful."

Noise began to jostle in the crowd, as the second band wandered up to the stage. The first note was a tube, squealing in pain. Then there was a deep bass, the notes like a water faucet dripping and echoing. And then it sounded like ten guitars, fighting each other, static around and behind and between. The music was the sound of people trapped in boxes, beating their fists against the wall. It was a gear, turning a crank inside my shoulders, then down to my hips, so I moved forward and back, side to side, not on purpose, but because the sound was churning my whole body. Vonn and I fought our way through the pit and flailed in front of the stage. When boys started flinging toward us, I just shoved them back where they came from.

18.

After the singer rasped "Thank you," and they all stumbled into the crowd, a set of lights turned the rest of the bar from dark to dim, while another round of cords was hauled off stage and replaced. I stumbled back to the restrooms, hearing parts of conversations.

The lock on the bathroom door was supposed to slide shut, but I had to crouch over my stomach, leaning far over with one arm stretched straight in front of me, to hold the door closed. The cramp was terrible.

Washing my hands, I looked white and scary in the mirror, sweat ratting my hair. I tried mechanically to fix it, scraping it down with my fingers.

"Are you okay?" someone asked behind me. I think her name was Laura.

"I think I'm going to throw up," I said.

"Let's go outside for a minute."

Out on the side steps, I was amazed at the existence of fresh air. I'd forgotten all about it. Contrast even made it feel cool. I leaned my head back and breathed. Cars went by, with the smoker's cough of missing mufflers, like missiles getting closer, then skimming the ground and disappearing. They were just around the corner, but really far away.

"I'm so sick of people talking about where they drank and what they did when they were drunk," Laura was saying. "You can't keep having the same conversation indefinitely."

I stared up at the sky.

"Everyone's so bored with the same old thing," she went on. "But the only reason it's the same old thing is because they keep doing the same things. They don't have to go to the same bar every night and then be bored because they're at the same bar."

"The only reason I go to the Egyptian Bar is because nobody will ever go anywhere else," I said.

"Exactly!"

Inside, they were still setting up for the headliners. A stand of lights onstage threw random flecks of red all around the room, temporary snippets of psychedelia splashing faces and bodies in the crowd.

"This is like Xanadu," someone said. I looked over, and it was the guy who sold pot across the street, in the back room.

"There've been statelier pleasure domes," I said. "But I guess we'll take what we can get."

"You know, it wasn't very stable," he went on, raising his voice as recorded music started pumping in. "Like shifting sands. It was built in air."

"Of course it was built in air," I hollered back. "He was a writer. Where else was he going to build it?"

He looked over at one of tables, their tops made of laminated jigsaw puzzles, big woodland scenes. Handcuff Girl was sitting on the edge, and her boyfriend, Tourette's Boy, rocked it like he was playing pinball with her thighs.

"I'm going to go see if they're in the market," he said.

"Beware, beware."

The opening band dawdled and delayed, while everyone drank and gossiped and the room fragmented into clumps of acquaintances, awkward in miniskirts and squeaking in leather. When they went on stage, the first thing they did was talk about how they wanted everyone to move their asses and get into the pit. It was their job to persuade me, not mine to please them, and I immediately went to the back to watch with my arms folded.

I wasn't the only one. Half the crowd sunk back to the bar, judging how much everything sucked. Laura was right. We were all so jaded, acting so smug and superior. But why not? Wasn't that the way of the world? Wasn't everyone judging us?

Besides, it was true. Most of the bands did suck. All the radio stations sucked. Thinking things suck is an art. We could have said that the government sucked, the job market sucked, the whole unfathomable system sucked. But what was the point of that? Better to pretend that the world was only messed up in our little corner. Thinking things suck is a dream that somewhere out there, things are better.

Or maybe it was just this band. They really did suck. In fact, they were terrible, and the singer flailed about, like he thought he was dancing.

19.

The next week dragged along, walking back and forth. Every day seemed a little hotter and drier than the day before. The prairie was faltering into a desert, and the word "dust bowl" came to mind. For a second I almost regretted my contempt for American literature; maybe Steinbeck would give me some insight. But then, I knew that times were hard and people were hungry. Especially me. I didn't like the sight of my rib cage, and my skin itched, like it was trying to shed.

I couldn't stand sitting in the apartment, so I kept walking around. I made a circuit of thrift stores, from the Salvation Army to the Little Old Ladies. Then I followed all the bike paths down by the trickle of river, past the huge swathes of mud baked to cracked clay in the hot sun. Some days, I walked gingerly down to the murky water and pulled a fistful out, trickled it along my hot arms. It left muddy tracks, temporary stains like watercolor water, but it cooled me off a little.

One afternoon, the sun still hot in the dirty sky, I followed the bike trail back. A few ten-speeds whirred by, but otherwise it was deserted. I passed into the shadow cast by the railroad bridge above me, and I heard a muffled moan. Sloping alongside me was a short wall of crushed rocks, like tombstones that had been smashed with a sledgehammer, and above them, going into the crook where the under-bridge met the ground, was a tall hill, just a dirt surface, not the crumbly powdery dirt, but rich and dark. A man was lying on his back on the slope, his shirt pulled up to mid-chest, his pants pushed down around his knees. His skin was smudged with dark dirt, muddy-looking, and he was slapping at his penis, hard, and grunting. I kept walking.

20.

"I pity the man who can see the connection of his own ideas. Still more do I pity him, the connection of whose ideas any other person can see."
— Thomas Love Peacock, *Nightmare Abbey*

21.

"Welcome, my friends," Dr. Bleak began. "The night speaks to us. It holds darkness over our heads, literally. And death, figuratively. People have always seen the stars overhead as hopeful and dangerous. Infinity bears down on us. The ridiculous redness of the blood as it pours out of your veins, the fine line between a laugh, and a choke, and a death rattle. The dumb look on your face when they cast your life mask. How quickly everyone will forget you. But we'll always have their pain to mock in consolation."

Dr. Bleak seemed to shift in his chair, a little uncomfortable.

"Many of you have asked why I say I have a Castle of Freaks. You may be the freaks I invite to the feast, but you don't think this looks like a castle. Well, I have a Castle of Freaks in the same way that Dr. Terror had a House of Horror. We don't cross the veil of time and eternity to broadcast into the earthly plane for people who don't know what a metaphor is."

I laughed out loud.

The credits couldn't have been any more 1970s. Plain lines of type, almost hand-lettered, saying "A Bankers Association, Limited, Production," and then a background frame of flashing faux neon. The word Disco appeared in big block letters, with a scrolling suffix, "teque," sprouting off horizontally. Then there was a knife slash across the credits and the word "Death" appeared in sloppy red over the word "teque," and it flashed over and over, "Disco Death – Disco Death." It might already be my favorite Dr. Bleak movie ever.

After a montage of flashing lights and close-ups of feet dancing in high heels, a girl with long blonde hair and a baggy tube top stumbled out of the disco, talking to the camera, which wobbled slightly, looking down at her breasts, and then back to her face, half-closed under garish blue eye shadow. The camera looked down the block at the line of people waiting, and then up at the neon sign reading "Sublime Discoteque."

Coleridge is spinning in his grave, I thought. Then I wondered, did it ever get to a point where they stopped spinning in their graves? Like at first, did things outrage them, but over time, seeing all the changes, did even the dead just give up?

"If you don't have any coke, I'm going back inside," she said. "I can find somebody who does."

A typical night at the Egyptian Bar, I thought. Guys would hold forth, superior, about where they could buy coke, and Jesus Christ, I knew where they could get it, and I couldn't care less. All they had to do was talk to some random dude in a Polo shirt.

The blonde girl went into a room marked "Private," where a guy in a fuzzy green leisure suit sat at a desk in a leather chair, and there was an awkward cut. Suddenly there was another girl in the room, wearing a spangly silver minidress, and I suspected she'd been giving him a blow job until she was edited for television. Disco music pumped into the room at a low volume, to give the impression that they could hear a distant dance floor.

"What do you want?" he asked, sounding bored.

"I never like to come by and not say hello," she said, flat, but obviously aiming for seductive, pulling her tube top over her head, with only her naked back facing the screen. The picture sputtered ahead again, and she moved behind the man, ran her hands through his hair. Then she held out the tube top in front of her, like she was about to wring it out in the laundry, and looped it around his neck. She pulled tight. The chair moved back with him. On the floor in front of him, the brunette girl settled back on her heels, her teeth instantly become fangs. The eyes of the two girls met, and they smiled. The brunette lunged toward his neck and a shower spray of blood spattered all over the wall and the desk, ketchup-bright red.

22.

My night life was a little less glamorous, and also short of vampires lurking in my usual spots. At the Egyptian Bar, the side door behind the pool tables was propped open, a giant propeller of fan wedged into the space. The room was half-empty, but somehow it felt crowded, people still too close.

"All these new people," an old-timer was griping. "We don't need them here. There isn't room."

"Head of a pin, man," someone said.

"Ahh, screw all that. The other ones are bad enough. The crap they've put on the jukebox."

"Come on. Maybe we should try to talk to them."

"Don't be ridiculous."

Just overhearing that made me want to find something to play, so I went and stood at the jukebox. There wasn't much I liked, but a few things were tolerable. At the closest table, the campus anarchists sat with their heads huddled over the table, two pitchers of beer between them. One of them looked at me suspiciously, as if I was interested in their plotting.

Suddenly, a penny hit me so hard in the face, I thought it would go right through my cheek to land flat on my tongue. I held the coin in my fist and glared around the room, trying to see who'd flicked it. Come to think of it, I hated the Egyptian Bar.

"Hey!" A girl in a long flowing dress called over to me. She wore several strings of colored beads and one long rope of Tibetan Rosary, the tiny brown skulls bumping around as she moved.

"Hey."

I didn't see Kim around that much anymore. She'd been in my survey classes, a slightly older-than-average student, as they called it, and had a little bit of that neo-hippie quality, but I liked her anyway.

"We're in the back room. Come and join us." Her face was warm and brown, just tingling into a sunburn.

I abandoned the jukebox and collected my glass, now mostly filled with melting ice, and a slight tint of murky alcohol. Vonn was deep in conversation, and we made vague gestures of explanation at each other, a directional shrug and a half-nod. Kim stopped at the bar and flirted shamelessly with the bartender, throwing back her long, rippled hair while he got her beer.

"Anything for you, babe," he said.

She leaned a stack of empty glasses in the crook of her shoulder, and hoisted the pitcher in the opposite hand. I reluctantly gave up my glass of ice to help carry another stack, and trailed to the back room. Her boyfriend Dale and a couple of friends had claimed the big table closest to the jukebox, which was strewn with lighters, cigarette packs, chunky glass ashtrays. Dale paused with a narrow pipe in front of his mouth.

"Hey," he said, welcoming, his voice strained from having just inhaled. "Want a hit?"

"No thanks," I said, setting down the glasses on the table. "I'll have a beer, though."

"Cool."

"It's great pot," Kim said. She started pouring the beer, hostessy. "I got it from my ex-husband. I have a whole bag at home. And a whole week off. The kids are at my mom's. It's heaven!"

"And we've been partying like the world is coming to an end," Dale said, laughing too. "Cause in a week, it is. We drove out to the lake this morning and we've been at the beach most of the day."

After a few beers, one of Kim's friends leaned into the table conspiratorial.

"Now you guys have all heard," she said. "People have been telling me that this bar is haunted."

"No way," Kim leaned back, cigarette at shoulder level. "I don't believe in that crap."

"You mean that this is haunted? Or don't you believe in ghosts at all?"

"Believing in ghosts is just the same as believing in God."

I motioned at Kim's crumpled cigarette pack, and she made an expansive gesture. I slid one out and lit it up.

"So what's the story?" I asked.

"All I know is that one morning one of the bartenders came in early to help, I don't know, unload some supplies or stuff. So she went into the back room by herself, over there." Her voice was hushed. "When she opened the door, that's when she saw the ghost."

"What did it look like?" Kim asked.

"And what was she smoking, and where can I acquire it?" Dale put in. They all laughed.

"She said it was a girl. It startled her because at first she thought it was a real person standing in the closet, like someone had been locked in all night. She jumped back, and without her looking away, the girl completely vanished."

"Oh, please, that is the most fucking Scooby-Doo story I ever heard," Kim said.

"Well, someone has to have seen a ghost at some point, right?" her friend said, stubborn. "Otherwise, no one would have ever believed in them."

"When people die," Kim said, like she was talking to a child, "their spirits just go wherever they're supposed to go."

"How do we know they go anywhere?"

"If they didn't, there'd be millions of ghosts, everywhere."

"Maybe there are," I said. "It's not like they'd take up any space." Breathing in, my lungs felt like they were clogged with ectoplasm.

I left early and stopped at the restroom: initials scratched into the metal doors, magic-markered words, stickers for bands that were dead and gone. Then I threaded through the growing crowd. The break between bands at the Jigsaw always filled up the Egyptian. A few people, scanning restlessly to see who they knew, called out to me and waved. I waved back, but kept going out the door.

In the lobby a girl was imploring the pay phone, half angry and half in tears.

"What's wrong with you?" she demanded. "Are you some kind of pathological liar? You promised me!" Her voice rose into a squeal of rage. "You think you're so fucking cool! It's pretty fucking cool to run away from your problems."

I turned sideways to avoid bumping into her. The girl pounded softly on the metal shelf under the phone. She smelled slightly like brandy, and more strongly of cigarette smoke. It was like her clothes had been soaked in failure. Just like mine, except they were beerier.

The night glittered outside. A group of kids in dark clothes huddled around the front entrance of the Jigsaw, and another group clowned around on the corner, making their skateboards swivel in the air. They shuffled their groups and folded into packs, shouting, jumping out of cars right on the street, while people yelled from the cars behind them. The front door at the Jigsaw was open, probably to let some air in, and a bang of chords, tuning up, bellowed into the street.

"I don't have a quarter, because my lousy friends wouldn't give me one," a kid in the scruffy cluster shouted toward another group further down the sidewalk. They all looked younger than me, and down and outer, hard as that was to believe.

"Have fun walking home tonight," a girl yelled. "Oh, that's right. You don't have a home!"

"Who needs it?" the boy said, confident. "I've got a job."

Just down the block it drifted into a quiet residential street, and I was sure the people who lived there must hate the Egyptian and the Jigsaw. Although they'd been there forever, so people must be used to it. Maybe some of the older folks at the bar lived around there. I'd never really wondered where they came from.

I headed toward a row of old apartment buildings, two stories high, that I'd always wanted to live in, but they were the kind of places where people stayed for thirty years. The windowsills were filled with the knick-knacks that old ladies kept: finely crafted plaster figurines, china plates propped up like clocks, things they didn't give to thrift stores. Sometimes, when a TV was on, I could glimpse in, and all the rooms seemed to be filled with real furniture, older than me. Wooden tables with doilies on them, candy dishes, framed black and white photographs of husbands in uniforms, probably dead.

Across the street was a looming dark hulk of church, which looked like a fairy tale construction, with a faux tower like a windmill and oversized brown shingles. It was probably supposed to represent something theological, but I had no idea what. At night, the details all blurred, so it just looked like a raggedy tower, almost like it was bending toward the street. That's Burke for you, I thought as I caught sight of the church, tall and steep and indistinct in the darkness. Maybe not quite sublime, but not the opposite either.

Since I didn't live in any of these apartments, though, I turned reluctantly and backtracked to Main, walking down its bleak length, where the modern world had done so much damage. There was no logical reason why something had to be ugly just because it was new, but it seemed to be the case. And people like Wordsworth had bemoaned the modern world all that time ago, and so did those antiquarians who looked back regretfully to the lost past, two hundred years ago. Had they seen what was coming? Or if they had known what the future held, would they have appreciated more what they had?

A burst of dust spattered in my face. Down the street, a whole dust cloud spun around, almost as tall as the buildings, then it spun into a collapse, fine particles dissolved into the air. It was like there were spirits in it, consciousness, ghosts that wouldn't wash away even if it did rain, which it wasn't going to. It was so muggy, my lungs barely even recognized it as air. The bright moon, pure white, looked like a cool, slightly fuzzy mirage, painfully beautiful over such a horrible world.

23.

I cut through the alley behind my building, around the garage units, which was a mistake. At night, the row of impersonal doors reminded me that anything could grab me, and no one would ever know I'd been there. It would be like I disappeared from the doorway at the Egyptian Bar. When I pulled open the door into the lobby, I was almost surprised to find my hand touching the metal, instead of the flesh going through it in a mist. It was just like when someone touches you and that wakes you up.

Without making any kind of decision, I pushed the button down when I got in the elevator. I guess it was talking about the Egyptian Bar being haunted, but I suddenly wanted to look in the laundry room. The overhead light in the basement hallway flickered, like a cheesy effect in a Dr. Bleak movie, and I remembered that one of those doors belonged to the creepy guy. Maybe he was standing behind a door right now, looking out the peephole.

I started to reach for my keys, but on a whim on top of the whim, I tried the door, and it creaked open, even though it was a door that locked, automatically, when it was shut. I leaned into the room, without actually stepping into it. The light from the hall filtered in, and I could see that the floor was damp. I scanned around the room, focusing. There. By the window. It looked like someone was standing there.

My brain didn't believe it was a real figure. There was no ghost in the laundry room. I knew that when I turned on the light, I'd see a weird shadow, or natural shapes in an unnatural position. But the more I stared, the more it looked like a person. I focused on the spot and switched on the light.

It flickered a couple of times, before the bulb flared into light. Standing there, clear and solid, was a young woman. It wasn't a sundress, but a floral housecoat, halfway between a robe and an apron. She stared right at me, but somehow I couldn't really see her face. I gasped. And I must have blinked, because then she was gone. I didn't see her disappear. It was as if I had turned away, and then when I looked back, she was gone. But I hadn't turned away.

The garish flow of light had hit the room. There were empty garbage bags all over the floor, flat green balloons, rags of plastic, lying in puddles.

I backed out of the room and slowly shut the door. I tried the door again, and it was locked, like it should be. Slowly down the hall, part of me wanted to run, but I stayed calm. There wasn't going to be any Orpheusing tonight, or any Lot's wifing, but there weren't any myths about listening for sounds. The elevator was still waiting for me, so it barely bothered to ding before the doors slid open. I glanced to make sure it was empty, and hit the circle for my floor as fast as I could.

I wasn't even sure what had happened. Was it possible for me to have negative capability, and not reach irritable after fact and reason? I trusted my brain too much to really believe I was hallucinating. But it wasn't a ghost before and it couldn't be a ghost now. This place was too nondescript to haunt.

24

One day the phone rang at six in the morning. I stumbled to answer it. I'd been at the Egyptian until barclose, so I felt pretty bleary, but I didn't hesitate for a second. I didn't even need to know what the assignment was.

My flea market coffeepot sat on the stove top. I filled the metal basket at the top with grounds, and its guts with water. As the water boiled, it thrust coffee up into the clear knob on top, visibly rushing in and out like a miniature washing machine. I could only tell it was done by the smell, and by then it was usually too late, and it was too bitter. But I didn't really care: it had one job to do, and did it.

Then I found one of my so-called work outfits, in this case an unflattering cream-colored dress with a top like a loose blouse, a floppy bow tie around the neck, all scattered with flowers. I scrounged in a dresser drawer for nylons, then the ugly shoes, and folded them all into my handbag.

I rushed the coffee down, brushed my teeth, pulled my hair into a black binder, which I was lucky I had, since actual rubber bands were frowned upon. Then I walked across the river, but this time I skirted the skid row.

The job was in one of the shiny office buildings downtown that obviously aspired to be skyscrapers, even though they were way too short. Alcoves on the street level set the entrances back as far as possible, with walls rising up to sheer windows, reflecting the street back at itself. When I found the right address, there was a slab of ugly sculpture in front of the door, twisted pieces of metal that seemed to be plopped down at random and arbitrarily tangled.

I needed to check in at a security gate, which was clearly ridiculous to get into a potato consortium. But I gave them my name and the name of the temp service, flashing the little plastic pocketbook the agency gave me: it held my time card, an embossed pen, their business card, and a tiny mirror, which would only come in handy if I ever needed to flash a message to somebody, which was unlikely.

The girl who met me in the office looked like the kind of person the temp agency assumed they'd be hiring. She was pretty, but she could have used the mirror, since her makeup was a mask of beige. It seemed especially unnecessary since she looked younger than me. She wore a long, shapeless cotton sundress, a pale, pallid pink, with a white blouse, shaped like a cotton t-shirt, underneath, and her curly blonde hair was pulled back in a ponytail holder, flourished with feather and crystal threads.

She immediately began to chat, breathlessly, about her thumbnail life story. She'd started out as an education major, but after student teaching, she grew deeply interested in the family potato business. This was her first time being left in charge, and she needed an assistant, at least for today.

My job was mainly to sit in a chair, in front of a minimalistic desk, its frame a yellowish wood that was thin as a sheet of cardboard, with thin slices of metal forming slots instead of drawers. On the desk was an equally skeletal lamp, made of thick wire, with very expensive-looking glass tulip cups sticking out of it. From the little lobby area, I could see two other doors, one which was closed, and had an imposing gold plate on it; the other was open, to reveal a cluttered desk with a bunch of Target picture frames turning their backs to me, and what looked like a crystal unicorn.

The girl told me how to answer the phone, and how to transfer a call, and then she disappeared into her office and closed the door. I sat there in the uncomfortable chair. I had brought Bate's biography of Keats in my bag, for whenever I had a lunch break, but I didn't dare just sit there reading it. So I scrutinized everything visible, which wasn't much. Within fifteen minutes I was already feeling crazy and claustrophobic.

After a while the girl popped out of the office and stood directly in front of mt desk.

"I'm working on a project," she announced dramatically. "People love tater tots, but I think the name is off-putting. They need a name that's zingier. Sexier."

Without the hint of cannibalism, I thought.

"So I've been tossing around ideas. You're an English major, right?"

I hadn't said anything about myself. I wasn't sure I'd spoken since I walked in the building. The agency must have told her that.

"Yes," I squeaked.

"Okay." The girl pulled a sheet of paper out of her pocket.

"Snack spuds."

There was a long pause. I tried to make a face like I was thinking about it, weighing the possibilities, and put on a "maybe" expression, hoping I wasn't overdoing it. I didn't want her to think I was being sarcastic.

"Spud d'oeuvres. Tater trims. Petite potatoes."

After each phrase I waited with an air of expectancy. I tried to keep looking ponderous. After half a dozen, I realized no more were coming.

"I like spud d'oeuvres," I said. "The word spud sounds kind of down home. But the d'oeuvres part adds sophistication."

The girl brightened up.

"That's my favorite. Although I think snack spuds is probably more marketable."

I nodded, grave.

"A lot of people can't spell hors d'oeuvres. And they don't like to eat things that make them feel stupid."

That was too much. She did think I was being sarcastic. But no, she just nodded, and flounced back in her office.

This time she didn't shut the door all the way, and I could hear her make a long phone call to somebody about who was at the Liquor Station last night, and how Jenny was crazy if she thought Mark was actually going to call her. Then somebody's boyfriend got in a fight. He'd already gotten in the car, but someone called him a chickenshit, so what could he do? He didn't really have any choice. The cops had come, and his hand was broken, and his parents were going to be so pissed. Halfway through the story, I realized it was her own boyfriend. She had to call him after lunch and see how he was holding up.

"My first day in charge and I spent all night at the emergency room," she sighed. "Listen, what do you think of snack spuds? No, it's a new name for tater tots. Of course you'd still have to cook them. Oh. Well, maybe we could pre-cook them. They'd be like potato chips, but shaped like tater tots!"

I tried not to look at the clock. I re-read the same memo, about how people had to stay in their own parking spaces, and not use other people's, even if they were in the car with the motors running, for the twentieth time. But even eternity passes, and the girl came back out of the office with a handbag dangling from a long suede string.

"It's time for lunch!" she said.

Nothing had been said about lunch or breaks, although in this case it would only be a break from arduous boredom. According to the agency, that was something the temp and the client had to work out between them, but here, neither one of us really knew what we were supposed to do.

"Here's some cash." She pulled some bills out of the purse and waved them, like a treat for a dog to jump for, and rattled off instructions about getting her a sandwich across the street.

I didn't know what was across the street, but I didn't ask.

I took the money and went out.

When I stepped from the glass confines of the front lobby, the air conditioned ice-cold gave way to a blast of dry oppressive heat. It was still a relief to be back on the sidewalk. I felt a vertiginous desire to just walk away. I'd be rich with twenty bucks. But I faced across the street, and the Businessman's Bar was staring at me, obvious.

I ran across the street and pushed at the heavy door. Cold hit me again and my bones felt a jolt of shock. Coming in from the hot noon glare, the bar seemed completely black, as if there were no lights on at all. It was like a sensory deprivation room, cold and very dark. With my eyes shut off and my skin numbed in the instant dunk of cold, my whole body tingled with the silence. The room was absolutely still, and then I heard whispers. The whispers seemed to fill the room slowly, from the corners, until my ears were full of them.

Then my eyes adjusted to the light, and I could see it wasn't black at all. There were dim lights above every booth, and a steady hum of conversation, the booths and the stools full of alien old men in suits. I must have been about to pass out, I thought. I hadn't eaten anything since sometime yesterday afternoon.

I blinked my way to the bar. The surface was a smooth polished green, inside a dark wood oval, and behind it, the bottles were clean and orderly, for calm, Scotch-drinking people.

"I'd like a vegetarian sandwich," I said. "Extra mayo, but no sprouts."

"What kind of bread?"

"Whatever is ... normal."

It was hardly worth worrying about it, for what the potato princess was paying for my time, but still, I wanted to be in good with the temp agency. I didn't want to get a reputation as an incompetent lunch-orderer. All the important lunch ordering that I might miss out on, if I played my cards wrong. When I brought it back without incident, I had to hem and haw a little until the girl realized that I was supposed to get a lunch break too.

"Take a half hour. Forty-five minutes. Whatever." Then she thought a minute. "Make it half an hour."

I didn't have anything to do for lunch, or any money, really, but I could use some coffee. I walked down the block to the drug store with the lunch counter, passing old guys on the street, wearing parkas in the sweltering heat, and a hulk of a man with an egg-shaped head. Another guy leaned against a peach-colored brick wall, his hair unwashed to stiff bristles, his skin pocked and pitted. He held out his palm, and mumbled a conversation to no one.

At the lunch counter, I got a white Styrofoam cup of coffee, two condom-packet-sized envelopes of non-dairy creamer, and a thin stir stick, fluorescent green. I swirled in the creamer, which settled, muddy, in the bottom of the cup, even though it was supposed to dissolve. This was more like clay, or the silt in the river that made it so murky and gray. I tried to fizz it up with the stir stick, but all that did was spread the muddy through the brown. But there was caffeine in it, and that's all that mattered.

I picked up a brown paper lunch bag of popcorn, too, and that was much better than the coffee. It was fresh and hot, yellow and slathered and buttery, but not too salty. Coffee in one hand, I strolled onto the sidewalk, using my tongue to pluck fluffy kernels from the top of the bag, eating them one at a time.

Downtown in the wanna-be city I walked past the skateboard plaza, where kids wheeled along the backs of concrete benches no one would ever want to sit in. I gulped down the coffee and threw the cup away in a spiky garbage can. It looked like it was trying to bite my hand when I neared its mouth.

25.

I was early to the Egyptian Bar yet, and only saw one familiar kid bragging about his new job across the street, like filling pitchers with beer out of a spigot made him a rock star. He always proudly introduced himself by saying that people called him Blondie, like Clint Eastwood. I didn't know what he was talking about, but fortunately I didn't give a shit. Now his hair was bright pink, freshly dyed, so I asked, "Do they call you Fuchsia now?"

"What?"

"Nothing."

He was saying that one of the kids who worked at the Jigsaw had died, but I didn't think I knew who he was.

"That's just a rumor," the bartender said. He had been pretending to clean the bar, humoring the kid, but not really talking to him.

"What's the difference?"

"A rumor isn't a fact, dude."

"You know he was a total druggie. His pupils were fucked. They were never going to be normal again."

"I have to agree, that doesn't sound like conclusive proof," I said.

"Swear to god."

"Hey, man, it's not cool to talk about how fucked up he was," someone said mildly. "Respect for the dead."

"Fuck the dead."

"I'm sure they feel the same way about you," I said.

"I heard he was in the river, too," someone added. "That's two guys in, like, a month. Creepy, right?"

"There was nothing in the paper about this," I said. "Or the news."

"Oh, he killed himself."

The bartender shook his head. He was one of the young ones, but they seemed to prematurely age, matching the old guys who'd worked there forever.

"Dumb punk kids can't run off to the cities where they belong anymore, without it becoming an urban legend."

I took my splurge of wine cooler to the booth by the jukebox, watching the haircuts come and go. Handcuff Girl and Tourette's Boy walked in, already arguing.

"Fuck you then!" he said, his voice piercing the room. I called him Tourette's Boy because he swore a lot, even for the Egyptian Bar, where the motto "Fuck you" could be printed on a coat of arms, maybe under a beer pitcher.

Click of pool balls, harsh laughter. A group of girls from the Jesus College huddled in one of the middle tables, watching Handcuff Girl as she swept elegantly by them. They looked out of place, since it seemed to be a scruffy hippie night. One of them was a mountain man, red face lost in his beard, wearing a dirty flannel shirt. He stalked around, mumbling at people. He'd say, "Help me out?" And he'd start to explain what he needed, but lost his train of thought before he got to the part about needing a cigarette or a couple of bucks. He wanted to tell his tale of how he ended up in this situation, starting from the beginning. And there was more to that than he was in a condition to handle.

He'd already wandered up to their table once, and their eyes had all wandered in different directions. One brassier girl said, "We're not interested." She kept repeating it until he went away, her crisp voice getting louder, the same thing she'd tell a telemarketer. He looked like he was going to go over there again, but instead he approached a knot of guys huddled around a pitcher in sullen silence, like they were holding a séance and the beer was going to give them an oracle.

The jukebox clicked over to Patsy Cline, a note of melancholy almost drowned out.

"I'm freaking out!" the hippie was saying. "Isn't it okay to freak out anymore?" He looked around for somebody to punch, angry at the passing of time. "You fucking kids. I've been coming to this bar since before you were born. I wrote half the graffiti in the bathroom."

"Good for you, Grandpa," one of them said.

"Yeah, good for me." He looked unstable on his feet, like he could tip backward in vehemence. "Someday you'll be freaking out. Remember that." He started to walk away, but turned to holler at them. "Remember that!"

26.

Hunger had caught up with me. It was an active force scratching my guts from the inside. I felt claustrophobic, and I could feel my bones. I rummaged through the cupboard, looking for something to eat, and was relieved to find a small bag of sugar and one of flour. I'd bought them when I first moved in, full of optimism, with a few bucks in my savings account. Nothing had turned out like I thought it was going to, but I guess I'd read some really good books in that time, so things could be worse. Anyway, I mushed up a stick of margarine and smoothed in sugar and flour, until it tasted like cookie dough. It was delicious.

An action movie was on TV, with the jitter of machine gun noise, and various things blowing up into staticky flames, the sound turned down. I settled down in front of it, the saucepan plunked on the floor in front of me, and I ate the dough by the spoonful. I felt like a queen.

The movie ended with exploding and embracing. There were a few commercials: one for a jewelry store, reminding us that all love depends on diamonds; one for Cornpopper's, repeating their irritating jingle. I was sweating like crazy, just sitting there on the floor, the box fan pointed straight at me, its full blast feeling lethargic. It hardly seemed to move the air at all, but there was a placebo effect.

When another movie started, I couldn't keep my eyes open long enough to read the title. I must have been asleep by the time the station went off the air. The thing about TV is that it's like the world coming right to you, so going off the air was like the pulling of a veil, and everything outside disappearing in a second, leaving you alone in your own life. Anyway, when I jerked awake, it was buzzing with low static, long gone.

A sound like a thud, by the window, seemed to have woken me up. My head startled up from the pillow I'd been leaning on, and I sat up, looked around the room. The light was still on in the kitchen, the saucepan still sat on the floor. Outside, the street lights flooded the empty parking lot. The world was dead and still. My head felt bleary. I got up to the bathroom, and when I was in there, door shut, force of habit, I heard a scrape from the direction of the kitchen.

Must be the neighbors. Or someone in the hall.

I stepped back out, turned off the lights and the TV, and lay down in the bedroom. I stretched out for a minute, and was just thinking that I needed to bring in the fan. Really, I thought it would be better to go outside and sleep on the dark grass behind the garage units. That's when I heard something again.

I poised to listen. Far away, in the ether surrounding the building, I could hear a vague sound, a distant humming, maybe the air conditioning unit next door, maybe something in the garages. I quickly ruled that out of my consciousness, focused down, and listened just to the silence in my own apartment. I caught my own breath, until I couldn't hear it, breathing so shallowly it didn't echo even inside my own head, in my own ears.

Then there was a jolt of sound, that caused me to jump. It was the refrigerator kicking in, its hum growling.

Jesus Christ!

It's not like I was a little kid afraid of the dark. Dr. Bleak had never given me nightmares, or made me sit up in the night worrying about poltergeists in the kitchen.

I lay back down. The room was stuffy. Under the pulled-down slats of the window blinds, the window was open as wide as it would go, but there seemed to be no breeze at all. The sheet was warm under me, like I was an iron, flattening and wilting it. I closed my eyes. I was going to get back to sleep.

Thump.

I crawled to the end of the flat mattress, hoisted myself back onto my feet. I looked over the room divider. Those blinds were still open, a vista onto the boiled bare street, so there was enough light to see that the room was exactly as I'd left it. Nothing was moving, nothing was out of place.

I had nothing even approaching a weapon, other than maybe hitting someone in the face with a Norton Anthology of British Literature. Of course, I knew there was no one in the apartment. I could see the whole thing when I walked in the door. One person barely fit in the shower, even when they weighed ninety pounds. No one could be hiding anywhere. And I knew I'd shut the dead bolt when I came in. It was a fact: there was nobody in the kitchen, or anywhere else.

The corner was a blind spot, but I went in and flared on the overhead light, filling the kitchen with a quick gasp of bright.

Nothing was wrong, nothing out of place. The cupboard I'd left open when I got out the flour hadn't eased shut. Everything was fine. I walked over to the front door and tested the lock. Of course it was firmly switched in place. Just to be sure, I reached for the jingly little chain and slid that closed as well.

Unless there was something locked in here with me ... but they'd have to be invisible. That wasn't a realistic concern. I headed back to bed, and when I walked past the kitchen, touched the light switch.

The moment the room went dark, I heard it clearly, a loud thud banging against glass. It sounded like it was coming from the bedroom now. The window had rattled a little from the impact. I went over, lifting the blind and peering out hard, first staring down at the sidewalk below. Impossible to tell. Then I stared into the ineffable distance of the sky, the layers of night, nothing to focus on, nothing to see.

I'm losing my mind, I thought. I went back to bed, determined to ignore my imagination. Despite the heat, I tried to pull the sheet over me, just for comfort, and then threw it off again. I fluffed up my pillow, that smelled, warm and sharp, of my own hair, my own shampoo.

There was a softer, almost imperceptible thump. A muffled thump. A tap that spread into a rub. Another gentle thump. I sat up, waited. I turned toward the window, got onto my knees. I put my hand on the string to the right of the window. My fingers ran over the bell-shaped plastic tip, to the two strings that pulled the blinds. I gripped them tightly and held my breath, without realizing it. At the next small thump, I yanked hard on the strings. The blinds flew up, and I half shrieked, jumping backwards, stumbling over my ankles.

In the center of the window, on the level with the window frame, was a head, large and almost lumpy-looking. I would swear, would absolutely swear, that it was the head of the creepy guy in the basement. And as I stared, it seemed to evaporate. In the first moment, it had seemed completely substantial, as real as anything in the room, certainly as solid as I was. Then it kind of faded, and became a mere shadow of a head, and then it was gone.

There was no one to hear me yell. I was glad, because of how embarrassing it would be. At the same time, I felt totally alone in the world. For a second, I wished I had a goldfish, something in the space with me, so I could know there was still something alive in the world. At least until morning, when suddenly the living reconstituted from whatever state they entered into when they went to sleep at the night.

I hauled the fan in, and the industrial hum began to overpower my heatbeat. I thought I wouldn't fall asleep, but I woke up, so I must have. My apartment was as shabby and as dull as it had ever been. Anyone I told what had happened would say it was a dream. So maybe it was. I didn't know who to believe.

I left the house early, and when I stepped out onto the sidewalk, instinctively glanced at the basement window, relieved not to see the creepy guy's head. Wind blew a brown gnarl of dirt in a moving cloud along the sidewalk, and it took me a second to realize there was an honest-to-god tumbleweed, wheeling right down Main Street.

The dust and dirt and wind went on and on, the ground was drying into a desert, and it seemed strange that everyone kept walking on top of it, acting like it was normal, when the world felt like it wanted to break out in flames.

Later I walked down to the Chicken Basket, and luckily, they had a special going on. They made tiny little chicken sandwiches, the chicken in a patty smaller than my palm, in a soft bun spread with tangy mayonnaise. The chicken practically melted, it was so tender. It was a feast. They were three for a dollar.

27.

On Monday, the temp agency called with an assignment that would start the next day. Someone had just quit. It was in the Industrial Park, a place I didn't even know existed, but I was amused by the name. Like an amusement park, only totally different. The office lady gave me a name and an address in some impossible area across the river, and I said I'd take it. I'd have to figure out some way to get there.

I walked across the river to the bus station and scrutinized all the maps. There was nothing helpful. The closest bus would still involve about fifteen blocks of walking. I tried to calculate how long it would take me to walk, if the map gave an accurate picture of the distance, and my best guess was that it would be about an hour and a half. So I'd better give myself two.

I got up extra early the next morning and made a pot of coffee. I gulped down the hot liquid while I scurried around with my clothes and my shoes, my backpack. The Keats biography was too heavy to carry all that way, so I decided on the slimmer *Recollections of the Lakes and the Lake Poets,* which I'd miraculously found on the book sale cart at the library,

Outside, it was still fairly coolish, and the ground even seemed slightly damp, like the grass had gone to sleep with wet hair. I'd dug out my old wristwatch, a present for my junior high confirmation—how long ago was that?—and I kept that in my pocket, although I don't know what I'd do it if took me too long. I walked down the main street, dusty with disuse. I walked across the river, the water far below, and a few old guys with fishing poles, sitting on the big cement drainage pipes, trailing their lines into the trickle of muck.

Then I walked past the liquor store we used to drive to from the dorms, on bitter winter storm nights, past the strip mall line of dentists' offices and storefronts selling orthopedic supplies and artificial limbs. The Knife and Fork Family Restaurant, a gas station, more empty warehouses, brick once painted white, now shredding and peeling, stone doorways filled with bird shit.

Eventually I angled off. These were more obscure streets, places where you could get a TV repaired and sell blood next door while you waited. Then I veered off into a residential neighborhood, the houses old and sometimes big, but getting rundown. Some of threadbare lawns were full of bright plastic swing sets and blue plastic pools, the water dirty, the turquoise innards beginning to sag; some had lumber and tools sprawled across their yards, sheets of plastic covering gaps in windows, and pieces of paper nailed to the front doors.

The street had sidewalks in some places and not in others. It would suddenly disappear, and then mysteriously there'd be pavement again. In the morning, the road was fairly quiet, and I felt conspicuous walking next to it. The trees were few and scraggly, and the flat bare flat dull of the ground was undisguised. Just flat and dull and mostly dead.

I entered the moonscape of the Industrial Park. It had been lying there alongside the city the whole time. Concrete pipes as long as a building stretched out in weedy fields, next to tangles of wire, shaped into bundles, like metal hay bales. The earth was bumpy with patches of dried concrete, some of the spots still wet, looking like the ground would cave in if you stepped on it. Trucks were parked everywhere, and all sorts of bigger vehicles I didn't know the names of. It was a corrugated world, the buildings low and sprawling, made of rippled metal and concrete blocks.

I went to a building on the far side, in a tiny cement building, dwarfed by its neighbors. The word JOHNSON was painted above the door in plain block letters, but there was no indication what kind of a business it was.

I was early, so I walked in circles, a block or two at a time, until other people started to get there.

Inside, there was a small paneled lobby with '70s fake leather chairs and an unused reception desk, with a small office behind it, where two women worked who were, as far as I could tell, the only employees. Or maybe they were the owners. The rest of the building was behind a partition: a big drafty warehouse, full of metal shelves, lined with paint cans. And off to one side, a row of fold-out tables and folding chairs. There were six of us there, and each of us had a work station that consisted of a bulky microfiche reader and a bulky computer terminal, with a heavy keyboard in front of it, flat on the table.

The women in the office barely noticed me. I could have been the same girl who'd just quit. One of them put me down in front a terminal and rattled off instructions on how to set it up. The other temps, all women, were going straight to work, while numbers and letters ran across the screen.

"First of all, I'm going to have you do these revisions," she said. "A revision means a change."

"I know," I said. Not even sarcastic, like I would in my normal life, just factual, but she still gave me a sharp look. Country music blared from a corner radio. It was just after eight o'clock, and it already looked like a long day, with a long walk back.

28.

"O fret not after knowledge—I have none,
    And yet the evening listens. He who saddens
At thought of idleness cannot be idle,
And he's awake who thinks himself asleep."
    — John Keats, "What the Thrush Said"

29

I went to the Egyptian with no particular plans. There was nowhere else to go. Vonn and James were going to the Dramarama Dance Club with some friends, and I wouldn't pay a cover charge to drink, even if I had the money, and their tales of the Dramarama always involved people sweating all over them, or watching future kindergarten teachers get so drunk they peed their pants.

Kim walked in the door, Dale trailing behind her, and she waved at me like she was jumping up and down.

"We're just stopping by," she said. "Come with us."

It wasn't even completely dark yet, but in the long dusky stretch. We walked the block and a half to the Anonymity Lounge, which perched in the center of the Space Age Drug Store Mall. I always kind of liked it, because usually nobody I knew was there, and it felt like a place where time had stood still, although I wasn't sure what time it was.

The walls were big brown panels, with a wicker-like plastic pattern you could practically peel off the walls, and beer ads stuck on top of them. It was thick with a haze of smoke, a permanent fog. We had barely settled in a booth behind the thick wooden doors, in the smoking section when someone started talking over a microphone. We had run into accidental bingo.

"You have got to be fucking kidding me," Dale said.

Kim drank a gin and tonic with chunks of lime as big as the ice cubes, the glass sweating on the wooden surface, and Dale hoisted a big amber mug of beer. I drank my water like I was a designated driver.

"My diet's been going really well," she said. "But it takes a lot of willpower. Dale thinks I'm too skinny." She gave him a shove, then vacuumed up a big slurp of gin. "Which, it's not possible to be too skinny."

"Yes, it is," I said.

"What would that possibly be?"

"You don't want to feel your bones," I said, authoritative. "It's like, if you're aware of the bones in your arm." I gestured, opening my arms to the corners of the room. "And you can feel the joints rubbing together. When that happens, you need to eat something. Your body is reminding you that it's a skeleton, before it's too late."

"Now I want to order a burger," she said, tapping out a cigarette.

Suddenly there was a bustle around us, and a couple of her friends turned up to join us. That was always going to happen with Kim. One of them dressed like she belonged at the Jesus College, with self-conscious earrings, and the other I recognized as the ghost story girl. I'd pieced together that her name was Terri. They gossiped about people I didn't really know, and spouted some opinions about bands that I disagreed with, but for once, I didn't care. I didn't even really pay attention to them. I felt good leaning back in the wooden booth, watching light reflect off a gilt Coor's beer mirror.

"You still want a burger?" Dale asked. "The kitchen is closing at ten."

"God, is it that early?" the hippie friend asked.

"I have a better idea," Kim said. "How about the Dairy Queen?"

"There's no beer at the Dairy Queen," the New Waver said.

"When did everyone's horizons become so limited?" Kim scoffed. "I mean, beer is great, but it's not the only thing in the universe. We can leave for five minutes to get ice cream. Which is also great. Come on." She pulled some bills out of her big macramé purse, glittering with rhinestones, obviously an exceptional thrift store find. "Cones for everyone! I'm buying."

Dale had left his car in the big dirt lot behind the Egyptian, which sloped down to the river. A dark patch of trees covered most of it, but glints of water flickered behind. The sky still had some midnight blue in the streaks of cloud, and the air felt like it had opened a window.

"It might actually be cool enough to sleep tonight," Kim said.

"This summer has been horrible," Terri agreed.

"Hey," Kim said then. "There's somebody down by the river."

"Hobos," Dale said, dismissive. "The bridges are full of them. Like trolls."

We stood for a second and peered down the hill. I couldn't see anything, and neither could anyone else. So we piled into Dale's car, me squeezed in the back seat with some strangers, like usual, literally along for the ride. The DQ sat on a busy corner, a small, square, retro building, just a few walk-up windows and an island of picnic tables with beach umbrellas over them. In front was a mob of bodies milling around, loosely separating into lines as the people neared the front. It looked like a riot could break out at any second.

We waited in the parking lot while Kim went to get the cones, mostly in awkward silence, until the two girls gave up and just carried on a conversation with each other. Dale and I sat in silence until Kim came back, five cones in a cardboard holder, and passed them out like the mom she was. I put my tongue to the white surface, and it was the most delicious jolt of ice cream I ever tasted.

Dale turned out of the lot onto the Main Street, which was starting to glisten under the pressure of all the cars, and the streetlights above. The radio had been on, but now he popped in a speed metal cassette. I wasn't sure if he was driving faster, or if my mind was playing tricks, syncing us up with the music. All of us had the windows rolled all the way down, so the air rushed in at us hard, and we had to shelter the ice cream from damage.

"Where to now?" he asked, turning off on a side street.

"Let's go to campus," Kim said.

We parked on the street down by the student union, and stumbled out of the car, laughing at nothing and shushing each other. A brick walkway snaked around the side of the library and into the mall lawn, a giant wedge of grass intercut with random walkways and spotted with ancient oak trees. The buildings looked empty, what firm, sturdy brick structures would be if they could be deflated balloons.

The lights glowed amber, and the leaves on the trees were full, shiny green turned almost black in the night, some of them goldened by artificial light, and everything was quiet, with a very faint insect hum in the background. For the last few years, this place had been my whole life, and I felt like a trespasser.

Kim picked a group of trees in the center of the mall and danced around the widest trunk, making Salome-like movements, while the rest of us flopped down on the grass and looked up at the sky. It felt muggy under the arching roof of branches, a dome holding the air underneath it. The moon, half-full and bleached white, was half-hidden, sneaking its face in. Ivy curled around the brick front of the English Department, just to tell me that I was where I was supposed to be. As good as Oxford, if you squinted a little, and had never been to England, and didn't really know the difference.

"We were talking about ghosts the other day," Kim said. "You've heard, right, that the English department is haunted."

"I heard there's a curse on the whole campus," Dale said, one-upping.

A sudden wind rustled the leaves overhead. The shift brought the moon more into view, its light infusing the ground. I lay on my back, staring at the Gothic arch above the locked English department doors.

"That actually sounds kind of plausible," the New Wave girl said.

"What is it?" Kim asked.

"What do you mean?"

"What does the curse actually do? Is bad luck going to follow us around? Will we get Master's degrees from substandard universities?"

"You have to finish your Bachelor's first," Dale said, dryly. He got shoved again. "Seriously," he went on. "It's a frat story. They tell it to pledges and then somebody jumps out and scares the shit out of them."

"I don't know," the New Wave girl said. "I know a lot of these stories are just bullshit that people make up. But don't you ever get a creepy feeling, like there's something watching you when you're alone? I don't really believe in ghosts, but I don't not believe in them either."

I thought about the ghost in the laundry room, and the head in the window, and how the weird things seemed to be accelerating, but that was just me losing my mind. So I said, "The dead communicate with us all the time." I pulled *The Recollections of the Lakes and the Lake Poets* out of my bag and waved it around. "What do you think a book is? Thomas De Quincey has been dead for a couple of hundred years, and when I'm reading this, it's just like sharing a pitcher with him. Nobody needs a seance to get messages from the dead. And I talk back all the time, when I write in the margins, or do a paper about them. It's only too bad that they can't hear it."

"Maybe there's just a delay," Kim shrugged. "Like the post office, instead of the telephone."

"Do you think ghosts stay behind because they like it here?" her friend asked suddenly. "Maybe they just don't want to leave."

"Maybe dying is like being evicted," Kim mused.

"It does cost a lot just to be alive."

The shadow of the campus hung around us. I lay back again, leaning on my elbows, De Quincey across my chest, momentarily feeling the presence of ghosts, like me, with nowhere better to be.

30.

Dr. Bleak said, "Outside, the moon is full, the night is melting in the streets, the hot wind is howling, the beasts are running wild. You can try to ignore them, but if they catch you, you'll be found in the morning with your throat ripped out. Again. But for now, you are among the chosen. You have found the spirits, and the spirits have found you.

"We of the spirit world are always with you, my friends. Because you are alive and oblivious doesn't change the truth of the situation, which is that we were here first. No matter when we lived, we were always here before you. And finding our bones in the floorboards won't lay us to rest."

My sweat chilled on my skin a little. He was speaking with such conviction.

"The living think we want to find peace. Do the living want peace? The living think we want to take revenge, or to warn our loved ones of danger, or get our bones onto sacred ground. They expect us to have motivation. But do the living have motivation? Can they explain their purpose in taking up our space?"

If there are ghosts, I thought. And the ghosts are just like us. The train of thought blanked out. What would that mean? Since people are trouble, that didn't sound very good. It would probably double the complications of life. Maybe more. After all, how many dead people were there? Jesus Christ.

"But enough metaphysical speculation. It's time for our film, the delightful shudder-romance, Lamia."

The movie had a shadowy, Hammer-esque feel to it, black and white, full of mist and fog, everything I loved most. It was about Keats, training in the pharmacist's office, which looked more like a mad scientist's lab from an old Vincent Price movie than something supposedly set in the 1700s. Then we saw him meeting Fanny, in a drawing room like a painted backdrop, and then he was in a room with a fireplace, writing, shadows flung on the wall behind him. And then he went out in a snowstorm to meet a woman, which made me wonder if this was set on the Eve of St. Agnes.

Of course, she was a lamia, and after she bit him, he began to waste away, losing his will, and he drained away into nothingness, until there was just a shadow oozing off of his bed, and a shadow of light that fell across his manuscript. His friend snatched it up, hugged it to his chest, and in the distance, out the window, far away, Keats embraced the lamia, having made his choice.

It wasn't clear if she was a vampire, exactly. Maybe a vampire is just a ghost that's a little more solid than expected, one that isn't just seen and not heard, a ghost with some meat on its bones. It would take a real exertion of will to keep a seemingly coherent form, and maybe that exertion sucked the life out of people around them.

It was weird, I thought. I'd never heard of a horror movie about Keats before. Come to think of it, I'd never heard of a movie called Disco Death before, either. Where the hell did Dr. Bleak get these movies from?

31.

Every morning at the warehouse we were assigned a stack of microfiche cards. On the cards were recipes for paint. Each one had a title, a handful of words that I think were the names of cars, and then a series of numerical codes, which meant nothing to me. Except for those revisions, our entire job was to type the info on the cards into the computer program, as fast as we could.

Day after day, I typed in paint formulas. Every afternoon we were ranked according to how many cards we'd entered. Before long, I was the fastest in the shop, which bothered some of the other girls, who were pointlessly competitive about it, but I couldn't care less. I needed to do a good job because I needed the money, and my hand blurred over the ten-key pad.

Some temps came and went. Mostly those were women with nice haircuts and matching blouse-and-shorts outfits. I knew they lived in nice houses, and they talked about earning a little extra for their kids' hockey. They didn't have to put up with any of this. But I typed like my life depended on it, while bad country music fuzzed in and out of the transistor radio.

I never actually understood what the business was. There was all that paint, but nobody ever came into the building except the mailman, and occasionally neighbors stopped by to chat. But they never had customers. We could hear the bosses' conversations, since the door was always open, making sure we clacked hard enough. One of them was getting married, which necessitated endless phone calls, and long conversations which, I could clearly hear, were about the pictures in brides' magazines. They never said anything about paint. Sometimes I wondered if we were doing something illegal, but I couldn't imagine what.

Occasionally they would walk through to make sure we weren't taking any unauthorized breaks. Every morning at 10:15, they announced we could take a break. It was always right on time, but we couldn't stop until they said so. The temps had to go outside to smoke, while the bosses smoked in the office. I'd go outside and lean against the building, reading.

Then we had an hour for lunch, when the boss ladies would shoo us all out and lock the building. Everyone drove to lunch, somewhere nowhere near the Industrial Park. I wandered around the war zone, puzzling over the mysterious equipment and the names of businesses, offering unimaginable products and unknowable services.

Several blocks away, past an empty field waving with greyish prairie grass, I found a convenience store. I'd buy a Styrofoam cup of coffee, the largest size, fortified with a few shots of half and half. Sometimes, after a payday, I'd buy a doughnut, and lick the bits of sticky chocolate frosting off the crumpled plastic wrapper. Then I'd walk back to the shop, sipping the coffee out of the little trapdoor in the plastic top. The wind blew like it had a grudge against me, walking on the strand of sidewalk, on the edge of a barren field. Fast food wrappers huddled in the tall grass, dirty, sinking into the dirt, like sod. I'd be the first one back to the Johnson building, and I'd lean there and read, and jot notes in the back of whatever I was reading. Right then it was a selected works of Coleridge, with a line drawing on the cover that made him look like the frog footman from Alice in Wonderland.

"Coleridge using the intellect (reason) to make sense of the metaphysical, which is not strictly reasonable. Rational, irrational, arational?" I wrote. I need to read that Bakhtin book, I thought to myself. Somehow the idea of the carnival seemed to fit in with the idea of the occult, both of them realms outside everyday reality. And since everyone talked about him all the time, I was pretty sure that if I didn't mention it, someone was sure to ask, "Hey, what about Bakhtin?" I couldn't check it out of the University of Refugees' library because I hadn't registered for fall classes yet, but when they were open, I was typing paint formulas, so it didn't really matter.

I looked down the street at the reverse carnival I was in. This is where people came to do practical things, so practical I had no idea their jobs existed, and couldn't recognize them when I was looking straight at them. It was all about pipes and steel, the unseen foundations. These people had fading American flag stickers on their cars. They were probably Republicans. Here, all my reading and my grades meant nothing; less than nothing, in fact.

When we closed up for the day, I'd been sitting in one spot, typing, nonstop, from eight to ten fifteen, ten thirty to noon, one to two fifteen, two thirty to five. All that time with my hands bent over the keyboard, fingers never stopping to pause except to flip over the file cards and reset the microfiche machine.

Walking back in the afternoon, it was always a lot hotter, and the narrow roads were full of trucks and cars, much more treacherous. The dust from the fields and the trucks threw up a constant fog of gravel. It felt like I'd brushed my teeth in grit. My throat was dry and clogged with it. Sometimes I'd cut across an unused railroad track, fading into the earth. It was a long time to walk and think, and I thought about my place in the world.

Was this a break from my regular life, an interval I'd look back upon as an example of how hard I'd worked, and how far I'd come? "When I was young?—Ah, woful When!" as Coleridge had said.

But what if I couldn't afford to go back? If I didn't finish school? I had to face the fact that even if this job lasted all summer, if I walked back and forth every day, the paychecks were slow to build up. I knew I should be grateful just to pay the rent, to get back across the river at the end of the day without being hit by a car, to have a can of Folger's. But school would be starting before long, and the monolith of tuition seemed so far away. Maybe it wouldn't be enough.

Then what? I never thought I was going to go anywhere, win anything. I'd stubbornly stuck it out so far, being myself, but someday stubbornness wouldn't be enough.

32.

There was a letter in the box, a thread from the outside world, a place beyond my hot apartment, the hot street, the warehouse. It was from Gloria, saying she was coming to town for a weekend. It was such a jolt of excitement, I realized how narrow my world had become. She and I had walked all over together, finding odd details, creating the map and naming the landmarks: the Anonymity Lounge, the Little Old Ladies, and, because they both used the same surname, we flipped two businesses we christened the Mortuary Burger and the Hamburger Funeral Home.

God, the Mortuary Burger. It was so delicious, the mix of ketchup and mayo squeezing out of the paper wrappers. I could smell it, taste it, as if it were real. There was only ramen again, but I could save some money, eat out when she got here, have someone I could actually talk to.

33.

"… the lost Scholar long was seen to stray,
Seen by rare glimpses, pensive and tongue-tied,
In hat of antique shape, and cloak of grey …"
— Matthew Arnold, "The Scholar-Gipsy"

34.

There's no poetry to doing data entry, or maybe that's a failure of the imagination. It was so isolating, it was like doing drugs and getting paid for it. I worked the keyboard like a race car driver, faster and faster, as if the slightest mistake and I'd crash. My wrists and my arms ached slightly at the end of every day.

Fresh batches of microfilm came in, and the job dragged on. The boss and her fiancé couldn't agree on the reception. She liked the VFW, he liked the Teamsters' Hall. She called every deejay service in the phone book and haggled, while we typed in the other room. I could feel the carpals squeaking.

I didn't talk to anyone all day, and then I didn't talk to anyone when I got home. Would I notice if I went mute? It seemed like I was fading away, and in Romantic terms, would that make me more ideal? The real could never seem to compete with the ideal. Becoming actual, bound into flesh, seemed in the poetry of someone like Keats like it was a kind of failure. Even Coleridge had his "Constancy to an Ideal Object," with its "only constant in a world of change,/O yearning Thought! that liv'st but in the brain."

Walking home, my bra stuck to my skin. I cut through different parts of town. Every spot was the center of the middle of nowhere.

I saved everything I could, hoarded my change, but I couldn't see how I'd pay tuition in the fall. School was all I'd ever wanted to do, and the only place I'd ever felt I belonged, just from sitting in rooms where we all had the same books on our desks. All those ideas I'd started out with, reading the "Rime of the Ancient Mariner," thinking I could come up with new theories about old poems, like someone hadn't written down every thought I ever had. I had been totally kidding myself. I might as well buy some matching pastel shorts and Polo shirts, get a fucking perm. But that wouldn't even help. I was going to end up an old woman under a bridge, wheeling around a busted shopping cart full of paperbacks that were molding and swelling with water damage.

"There's the Professor," kids would laugh at me, and I'd point at them and holler, "You're going to fail someday too. Remember that!"

The skinnier I got, the faster I typed. The bride-to-be halfheartedly complimented my work one day. Otherwise, none of them really seemed to notice my existence, except when they saw me reading by the locked door after lunch, and they seemed to shake their heads a little.

I'm not going to lie. The more I thought about the future, the worse it looked. If I didn't go back to school, I'd need to find a longer-term job. This was the only job I'd been able to get. And the bride was right. I was good at it. My fingers flew over the keys, and my rent was going to get paid. It was pointless, monotonous, mind-numbing, soul-killing. Still, I could do a lot worse.

This could become my real life. I'd never fit in, not with the book-reading, but if I got in good with the temp agency, maybe I'd get lucky and move into the floppy bow-tie blouse jobs, like the one at the law firm. I hoped the pre-law student they hired was doing a terrible job, fucking up their copies, ruining their expensive machine. I hoped she was out at the Liquor Station every night and coming in with terrible hangovers, putting important documents in the wrong pigeonholes.

Maybe I should just save up all I could and move to the city, where I could probably make more money in Data Entry Hell than I could here. Maybe I could write articles for The Wordsworth Circle and come out of nowhere as a self-taught scholar.

Wasn't there a poem ahead of me on that too? "The Scholar-Gipsy"? That was the Victorians. We hadn't studied it in class, but it was in my Norton Anthology, and I'd read that from cover to cover.

Scholar-Gipsy didn't sound too bad. But without school, what was I? One of the countless people who'd lived, who were alive now, and nobody knew about us and nobody cared. The planet was full of me. I was a cliché.

35.

Thank god that Gloria was coming into town, a pretense of normality, like it had been during the school year. It was the first thing I'd had to look forward to, other than getting out of the house. When the day came, she called and asked if I could meet her at the Egyptian, with the friends she was staying with. "You'll like them. Or you'll get used to them, anyway." She was calling from the phone at the bar. I couldn't believe she was already there.

"Hey," she said when she saw me, sitting casual at the table by the pool table, surrounded by people, a whole gaggle. A couple of them were familiar, friends of hers from home I'd seen at the Egyptian Bar before.

"Hey," I said. She did a hasty introduction, pointing in random directions.

"I haven't been here in two months," she announced. "And you know those guys?" She nodded toward a pair of campus anarchists, huddled in a booth. "They were sitting in that exact same place."

"I bet they were wearing the same clothes."

"So how are you doing?" she asked.

My eyes flicked around the room for a second, like it had information for me. "Good. Everything's going great."

"Good," she said. "You know how I didn't want to go back home this summer, but it's been really a blast."

A couple of guys in t-shirts from the Science School thudded pitchers down on the table. They seemed to have been talking about Pink Floyd.

"Have some beer," they urged. "It's on Uncle Sam."

"In that case," I said, and accepted a glass of exceptionally yellow fluid.

"They're friends of Kevin's," Gloria leaned over to me, quietly. "He doesn't want us to get into politics."

"I'm not getting into anything."

"Here's to the Army," one of the guys raised his mug. "I couldn't afford to smoke pot without it!"

He halfway noticed I was there and asked, "So what do you do?" blearily polite.

"I work in the industrial park," I said.

"Doing what, driving a forklift?"

I raised my hands and whirred my fingers over an imaginary keyboard. "Data entry," I said. "Paint formulas."

"Pain formulas?"

"Same thing."

The End Times guy, the old dude, was making his way through the bar, pushing away invisible people. People scowled at his dirty clothes. "Can't you see them?" he was saying. "This bar is crawling with them!"

"I see that guy everywhere," I said mildly.

I started telling Gloria about Dr. Bleak, but she just sort of uh-huhed me. I was glad I hadn't mentioned the severed head.

"You know Karla's in town too," she said. That was a girl we'd hung out with some last year. She was in the Creative Writing program, so we really looked down on her from our Brit Lit heights, but not to her face. I suddenly wasn't sure if hanging out with Vonn and James had made me ruder, or if Gloria had made me two-faced. "We're going with her to a keg tomorrow, by the Science School. You have to come."

I just stared at her. She had said that with a straight face.

"Are you talking about a frat party?"

"No, of course not. I don't think so. It's somebody's apartment, some of Karla's friends."

More people started cramming in. I'd thought we'd get away for a while, go down to the Mortuary Burger, actually talk, but I felt my fate was sealed. I winced down another beer.

Behind us, a couple of the old timers started a game of pool, and while Gloria and her friends hubbubbed around me, their conversation came through in an undertone.

"This is the worst drought I've ever seen," one of them said. "We've had bad summers before, but I don't remember the river ever being so low."

"People think we could never have another Dust Bowl," his partner replied. "Shit, did you see the wind blowing on Main this morning? It's happening all the time."

"North side of town, they've been shorting out the power grid. Too many air conditioners running. Can you imagine, if all the power blew, in this heat?"

Somebody laughed. "I'd like to see these kids cope with that."

36.

Gloria didn't offer me a ride to the party, and I wasn't going to ask. When I walked over the river, it was a strange time downtown, a pre-dusky silence. The businesses were closed or closing, the streets emptying, all the daytime bustle fading away into shadows. Gray people sat on useless bus benches, at corners where buses didn't go. The light shifted and slanted with the long-falling evening.

I walked past the Art Deco Theatre to the Railroad Used Books, a warehouse next to the tracks, jammed with years' worth of books in cardboard boxes from floor to ceiling. I went down the narrow aisles, around the obstacle courses, to the Literature section.

Used bookstores are usually overflowing with dull American literature, especially when you hit the evil patch of the alphabet full of Faulkners, Fitzgeralds, and Hemingways. I got past that to a shelf full of fat Norton Anthologies and slim Dovers of random Victorians, and then chanced upon the Riverside edition Byron's Don Juan, its cover smooth and almost silky. I had loved how mean Byron was to all the other Romantics in that "English Bards and Scotch Reviewers" poem. We would clearly have gotten along.

Obviously he'd have been an annoying trust fund snob, but he seemed like my kind of bitchy. I snatched the book off the shelf and put it to my nose, breathing in, probing for the smell of must or mold. But it was fine, so I dug into next week's doughnut money.

The party turned out to be at Ryan and Bill's. They were in American Lit and lived with some old friends near the Science School, in a row of houses full of guys just like them. I'd say they weren't as low on the spectrum as Karla, with her sad John Cheever dreams, but really, past a point, it was all more or less the same.

Normally I tried to avoid Everclear and fruit punch, even separately, but it was there and it was free, so I felt duty-bound to drink it. At least they weren't taking whatever mismatched alcohol they had and pouring it into a garbage can, like some parties I'd been to. I had my cup in one hand and Byron under the other arm, and a Jesus College-looking girl said, "Gee, I forgot to bring my homework to the party."

"That's too bad. Reading improves the mind."

"What is that, Brit Lit?" She made a dainty sneer. "I'm in World Lit. We're reading *Hedda Gabler*. Strindberg is a true master."

"Ibsen."

"What?"

"Henrik Ibsen. He wrote *Hedda Gabler*. Ibsen was Norwegian; Strindberg was Swedish. Both had the bleak Scandinavian world view we're so familiar with here, but Strindberg was more fun. He was a total nut." I warmed up. "He had this whole thing where he was basically stalking his ex-wife on the astral plane. And he'd send her letters like, last night we had sex on the astral plane, and now you won't even return my calls! And his *Inferno* is fantastic."

"Dante wrote *The Inferno*." The girl's voice was tightening. She didn't know me. If provoked, I could do this for days.

"*The Divine Comedy*, yeah. Strindberg's *Inferno* is about his nervous breakdown. He thought people were after him, like the people upstairs were doing things to drive him crazy. So he'd move, but they always managed to find him, and move in upstairs again. It's a great book."

Luckily Gloria and Karla appeared. Karla swooped me into a hug, and they dragged me over to the stereo, arguing about what record to change it to. We wandered from room to room in shifting groups. It was a pretty big apartment, scarred from use by generations of Science School guys. Eventually Karla cornered me and started talking really fast.

"I haven't seen you in forever," she gushed. "Isn't it great not having to go to class? Although knowing you, I bet you're reading everything you can get your hands on. But I actually can't wait for school to start. I decided to run for Student Senate."

I said something in a vaguely encouraging tone.

"It's for my resume," she said.

I must have looked like a cartoon face, because hers turned sharp. "You know, you have to get serious about life eventually."

"We're at a keg," I pointed out.

"I'm not going to grow old and die this second," she said. "But we all want careers, and to have real lives someday."

I looked around the room. I don't know how many people were crammed in the bedroom. The Everclear must have been reaching maximum velocity. Everyone was talking at once. I could tell they were in the habit of eating.

"What makes this not real life? Is it a dream? An illusion?"

"Everybody can't be as high and mighty as you are."

"Everybody doesn't want to be a yuppie."

Gloria staggered over and pulled us into a drunken hug. She looked completely oblivious to the world around her.

I caught a ride back to the Jigsaw with a couple of Siouxsie Sioux girls. I saw them often enough, and it seemed like I should have been friends with them, but we weren't, for no real reason. As we were leaving, suddenly all of Gloria's friends became really effusive, and said how sorry they were that I was leaving.

We parked near the river, and walked around alongside the auto parts store. Just before we turned the corner to the main drag, I stopped. It was like a fist turning around inside my stomach, my esophagus wrenched and strained. I threw up right on the sidewalk, and they laughed.

"Shouldn't have drank the Everclear," one of them said.

"I shouldn't have either," the other said. She dug a tissue out of her vinyl bag and handed it to me.

"Words to live by." My face felt swollen and red. "You should never drink the Everclear."

"You still coming?"

"Of course." That's how it works. You throw up and you just

keep walking.

Inside, I rinsed out my mouth and spat into the sink. The bathroom throbbed dully and steadily with the music, vibrating expectantly, like I could expect it to launch into space. I didn't even care who the band was; I was going to dance until my bones fell off the joints. Some nights the pressure of other people in front of the stage was an exhausting weight. But sometimes it felt good, fighting through a crowd to a spot on the floor, to take up space and prove I existed.

37.

I spent most of Saturday at a table at the public library, in the air conditioning, reading. Gloria was supposed to call, and I didn't want to go to Perkins with them, watch them stuff whipped cream pancakes in their mouths while I ate buttered toast, and they talked about their jobs at the mall back home and their nostalgia for how drunk they were last night. But I met them at the Egyptian for a little bit, early that evening, before it got to Saturday night. Apart from us, it was mainly the old guys, pacing and shooting pool.

Gloria was drinking the terrible bar coffee, fabric wadded up on the table in front of her. "It's so great they're selling t-shirts," she said. "We all bought them. Everybody who comes here, we're like a family."

I just stared at her, and then I said, "Awesome."

38.

"Anyone who thinks death is nothing to joke about has obviously never been dead," Dr. Bleak started. His voice seemed particularly resonant, digging into the rich juice of his speech. "We all have so much to learn, on both sides of the veil. Spirits want different things, just like people do. In the movies, they always want their bones laid to rest. But writers and artists, they don't ever want peace. Their works are their bones, and they want their ideas to haunt the world, forever."

I looked around my room, at the stacks of books I'd worked so hard for, a thread of connection to Coleridge and Peacock and even Wordsworth, no matter how much shit I gave him.

"Tonight, at the witching hour, the air is still. Silent as the grave. You know that the ghosts are outside, looking in at you. The last ghost is the one in your lungs, in your bones, the ghost you will be someday. You can't hide from the spirit world, and you can't escape the ghost in your heart."

The movie began with a long monologue. It sounded like a continuation of Dr. Bleak's, but it was spoken by a young, handsome doctor, giving a lecture in front of an anatomical chart and a pile of books with "Ghost" in the title.

"There are all kinds of phantoms," he explained earnestly. "Most are content to echo, to sit in the places they used to sit, stroll in a garden, linger around loved ones and watch, puzzled, as they grow older, while the ghost, always, gets left behind. Death has its disadvantages. Some get angry with the state they're in, but they can't get back what they've lost. If they're determined enough, they can formulate their will, shape their energy. Just like with living people, a lot of time they put more energy into their spite than into their desires. More and more, troubled spirits, who used to be confined to a single location, are now wandering around the earthly plane, haunting anyone they come across."

The picture was slightly fuzzy, black and white, traveling quickly up to a filmy black curtain. When the curtain was swept away, suddenly it was as if I were looking through a pair of empty eye sockets. The camera backed away slightly, pulling us out of the skull enough to see where we were, and then moving forward, the field of vision swallowing the shape of the skull and just seeing what the skull was seeing: a fuzzy silent movie-style screen, with indistinct white letters: *Fugue*.

There was a fast pan through a hall of mirrors, then a close-up of a girl's face, frozen in terror, a scream stopped in her throat, her mouth wide open. Then a fast pan down the strange corridor, and shadow hands, shadow bodies fleeting toward her, clawed hands reaching out of misty air, and a ghost with a noose around its neck. The grays had a strange, overheated look, like they were supposed to be saturated Technicolor, but something had gone wrong at the last minute.

The story unraveled. A small town was being plagued by demonic beings, but they didn't materialize or appear in a tangible form. Instead, they seemed to come alive inside people. They bided their time and crept into people's skins, through their pores while they were sleeping. And then they destroyed them from inside, pestering them with guilt and despair. One of the characters was a teenage girl who had gotten involved in political causes, very sixties, and suddenly realizing the futility of trying to make a difference, took an overdose of pills.

When she woke up in the hospital, she tried to explain what was wrong, but nobody understood. Her parents thought it was about school, or maybe a boy, and they didn't believe her that she would feel so badly about such an abstraction. But it made perfect sense to me.

"Someone has to pay," she said.

"For what?"

"For everything."

Fortunately, the handsome doctor believed her story, and they went to a strange occult shop in Greenwich Village to meet a "reverse medium." He was dead, but he had a talent for communicating with the living world.

"When did your trouble begin?" he asked.

It was when an old house in her neighborhood got torn down, to build a new one.

"Where do the ghosts go when the house is gone?" she cried, a little hysterical. "What do they haunt then?"

Then it became more convoluted, with a whole conspiracy of ghosts, who believed that because all the living would eventually die, they should move the process along.

"It's better for them!" the ghost cried. "It's inevitable."

"Nobody understands the problems of the dead," another of the ghosts said, probably as self-pitying as she was when she was alive.

They were sort of like "pro-life" ghosts, I thought. Or maybe the opposite. But in their terms, they wanted the living to be born into new lives, as ghosts. In a way, it's like they were trying to reproduce, and the only way they could do that was to bring more death into the world.

In the climax, full of tilting camera, the girl stood on the edge of a convenient cliff, ready to throw herself to the waves. She'd decided that the ghosts were right all along. At the last moment, while the discordant soundtrack echoed the organist, the doctor and the reverse medium appeared together to save her, using an incantation to push the ghosts back under the ground.

Good for her, I thought, but it was no use counting on a Deus ex Machina in real life.

39.

"The sole true Something—This! In Limbo's Den
It frightens Ghosts, as her Ghosts frighten men."
— Samuel Taylor Coleridge, "Limbo"

40.

"Maybe Gloria will change over to American Lit," Vonn said. "It would suit her personality more."

It started nice and slow and dull at the Egyptian Bar: Seed Cap Dude at the bar, the silent Army jacket girl by the side door. James had almost been startled to see me.

"I thought you'd become a recluse," he said. "You haven't come out in ages. What's new with you?"

"Well, Keats is beginning to annoy me," I said. "That's all my news."

I still hadn't totally decided if James was more a Wordsworthian or a Keatsian. He obviously wanted to be a Keatsian, hence the running around with Vonn. But underneath it all, there was something stick-in-the-muddy about him. Wordsworthians were likely to think a little more highly of themselves, which suited him, although I have to say, professors tended to like us Coleridgeans better.

The Keats and Shelley kids, on the other hand, tended to be a little immature. There was something about the poets who died young, full of unfulfilled promise. When their fans didn't die young and leave a beautiful corpse, but aged past their idols, it was easier for them to settle down, become normal, and be embarrassed about their former effusiveness.

"How can you have anything against Keats?" he asked.

"You know, we always have to hear about his problems. He was so poor, and so struggling, and all that bullshit. But he could have gotten a job. He had opportunities."

"Keats was a genius."

"Well, sure. But it's like a guy in a band. He doesn't want to get a job because he wants to devote himself to his art. That's fine. But he's gotta eat, he's gotta keep a roof over his head. So he leeches off people and thinks he's better than they are. The world doesn't owe them a living."

"I think the world did owe Keats a living."

"Oh, please. There's lots of geniuses out there starving to death. And the more I think about this whole negative capability thing, I don't see that he's entering into any other consciousness, any more than anyone who's taking on a persona. Just because he fucking said so. I could say I know what this table is thinking, that I can put myself in its place and lose myself, and maybe talk you into believing it. But it's just making shit up, like every other writer in the world."

"Geez, you're harsh."

"Well, I mean, some of Keats is okay. 'Lamia' 's okay."

"Oh, 'Lamia' is okay." He dragged out the word. "Not great or anything, but it's okay."

Vonn had just looked amused. Later she checked to see that James was talking to someone by the back room, then leaned over, lowered her voice. "You better watch yourself around James. The meaner you are, the more he likes you."

"I've never been mean to James."

"Mmm." Her face was annoyingly knowing.

"I guess one of the old-timers died," James said, coming back to join us. "Just the other night. He'd been here playing pool."

"Weird," I said. "I saw them. We were sitting right at that table." They all looked like they were on death's door to me, and I probably didn't look any better.

"Old dudes die all the time," one of Vonn's black leather friends said.

"His spirit's going to keep sitting right on the same bar stool," his buddy added.

"And lots of young babes will be sitting on his lap."

They laughed, clanked their mugs together.

"I wonder if we'll live to be old-timers," Vonn said.

When she asked about my job, I just waved my hand in the air, "Oh, you know. There is an infinite number of paint formulas."

"I'm re-reading Shakespeare," James said. "And I realized something. None of the tragedies would have happened if the answering machine had been invented. So I don't know if they're really tragedies, or just bad luck."

"I'm not sure it would have helped King Lear," I said.

"Well, some tragedies are more tragic than others."

I leaned back in my chair. I felt like I was a complete stranger, like I didn't even live here, like I'd just gotten off a bus and stopped in the first place I saw.

There were buzzes of movement, hectic talk, all these people clutching some meaning out of this place, when most of them were probably the same as me, just going out because they couldn't stand being home by themselves.

Fuchsia wobbled over to our table, wearing a t-shirt with a big anarchy sign on it. Working at the Jigsaw was punking him up, at least superficially, which, frankly, almost qualified him to be in a local band.

"Are you serious with that shirt?" Vonn said. "You people all know that anarchy is doomed to failure, don't you?"

"People always say that," I said. "But I don't think anarchists care."

"Wouldn't that be a nihilist?" Fuchsia asked, guileless.

"There are shades and degrees," I said. "You know what William Blake would have made of all your defining and classifying."

He started to sputter, but Vonn convinced him I was teasing, putting her hand on his arm. Before long, he and James were arguing over the definition of cool.

"In any given situation, the coolest thing is always something that no one's ever heard of," James said. "For example, no bar could be cooler than one that doesn't exist." None of us could argue with that.

Che Guevara Guy came into the bar, and he seemed a little agitated. Vonn put her finger to her nose, and sniffed, giving me a little grin.

"Hey, what's up?" she asked, turning in her chair.

"It was probably nothing, but I thought I saw something down by the river," he said.

"Like what kind of something?"

"Well," he hesitated. "You'll think I'm crazy."

"I already do," Vonn said.

He grinned, half-hearted. "It was like there was a group of people, but they were flickering in and out of existence."

"Just like my building," I said, as if that were a completely normal thing to say, or anyone knew what I was talking about.

"It's dead in here," Vonn said. "Let's go look!"

What the hell. It was nice to go outside. We turned out backs to the Egyptian/Jigsaw corner, already gleaming with neon, and headed toward the back lot and the slope to the river. Behind that, a train was going by, and the whole town shook with the vibration. Through the darkness, we could see some bums sitting on a flatbed, shouting and swinging their bottles at us. We waved back, like we always did when we saw them.

We followed Che down the slope.

"I don't see anyone," Vonn said. Her voice seemed to ring out, twice as loud as normal.

"I think this was a ploy for him to be alone with you," James murmured to her. "He didn't count on your entourage." She snorted.

He'd gone on ahead, and we caught up with him, the other side of a muddy bike path, so we were looking down on a line of smashed rock and exposed tree roots that that lined the low bank. I peered down at the river. It was so dry, there was barely enough water to drown in.

"I don't see anybody," James said.

"Maybe they flickered right out," Vonn said, straight-faced. They all walked ahead, laughing, even Che, who had relaxed a little, thinking whatever it was, it had gone. I stood by the river, breathing in the earth through the soles of my feet. The air was cooler by the water, like the dirty sun would never rise again and ruin my day, and I didn't see any mosquitoes. Everything was accidentally perfect.

Then I looked back up the riverbank. The dark bulk of the Egyptian Bar, the street running past it, the town piled up on the other side, all seemed to lean and bear down, like it was all going to fall down the hill and crush me.

Or like someone was watching, had been following me. Not me on purpose, in particular, but just because I was there. The hollow under my ribs began to gnaw again. I could hear the low rush of the bit of rapids slightly upstream and started walking in that direction. The sound seemed to sync up with my heartbeat. It was like a faint whisper, in the back of my skull. Maybe I was kind of drunk, but it seemed natural to sense a voice drawing me in a direction, toward a lower point in the earth. I noticed it had gotten a little foggy, strange with everything so dry for so long, but it hung around the shrubs and trees and the underside of the bridge as if it lived there.

The only reason I kept going was because I was set in motion in the first place, just going toward more of the same, over and over. What was the point? I could work hard and struggle, but where did it end? Nowhere.

An image of Coleridge, thinking the same thoughts, only in better words, popped into my head. That made me feel worse. All those centuries, and nothing had gotten any better. We'd just gotten more inarticulate.

The low water almost glowed, and it was black underneath, not its daytime shade of filthy pewter.

It felt like when you're up so late, you're so tired, that you can't get to sleep, and you feel heavy, like your body is dreaming without any help from your brain. I felt like I could slip away from my life without even noticing. What would somebody like me haunt? I wondered. Someone with no particular place.

Coming here was a mistake. The temp agency was a mistake, this town was a mistake, and the University of Refugees was a huge mistake, and all the jobs I ever had, every guy I ever talked to, the way I'd dealt with everything, and I went backward trying to find something I could say, without any reservation, wasn't a mistake. But I couldn't think of anything I could have done instead, that wouldn't have been a mistake. So I wasn't even sure it was my fault.

If I went into the water I'd become invisible, and that sounded so nice. Like cooling off in a bath after this hot dry night. It looked like I could walk across the water. Moonlight skidded off its sluggish surface. It would be so much easier to walk into it, the voice seemed to invite me. I could go into the surface, like a doorway into another room, and lie down under the water, in the silty riverbed and sleep, a real sleep, deep and full.

Suddenly I realized that someone was hollering at me. I was standing, about to step into the water. I looked back, expecting it to be James, but it was the old guy in the seed cap. I recognized him from the bar.

"You wanna get away from there," he said, taking a few steps toward me.

"Why?" I asked. It was the most sincere thing I'd ever said out loud.

I could see a half-smile in the dim light. "The river isn't going anywhere," he said. "You've got better things to do with your time."

A sudden whip of wind, like the night was hissing, and for a second, I could see them. Che Guevara Guy wasn't wrong. They were everywhere. The air was so foggy with ghosts I could barely see the bank of trees that was huddled right there. There were ghosts under my fingernails.

We sat on the riverbank, almost flat with the water, mist deep around us now.

"The river's just where they find you," he said. "It's not really where you die."

"Where do I die?" I asked, like I understood what he was saying.

"You die here," he said, completely conversational. I couldn't see figures in the mist anymore, if I ever had, but it pressed damp against my face. Vonn and James and Che had disappeared beyond the wall of white, and the Egyptian, the town behind, were gone like they never existed. "In the fog, surrounded," my thoughts trailed off.

I could feel it all around us, an endless unhappiness. It was like all the old-timers at the library, the guys on the train, I'm-Freaking-Out Guy roaming the Egyptian, trying to catch up with his buddies, find his keys, find his wallet, forever. We sat side by side, quiet, and then Seed Cap Guy hoisted himself off the ground.

"Come on up and have a beer," he said.

It all started to fade away. I headed up the bank, pointed at the deep charcoal sky, and of course, he was gone with all the rest of them. The moon hung white and salty and round, almost blasting me with light. At what point does the air become the sky? I thought, light-headed. It goes all the way down to the ground, but nobody thinks it's sky we're walking around in.

"Jesus, where did you disappear to?" Vonn asked, bustling up. "You freaked me out. I was hollering for you."

"We didn't see anybody," James said. "Surprise, surprise."

"That's good," I said. I still felt like I was dreaming, and it had permeated my voice. "I lost track of you in the fog."

"Fog?" Vonn asked, genuinely confused. "Are you stoned or something? You are literally the only person I know for whom that would be out of character."

"Who can afford that?" I said, sounding like me again.

"You are stoned," she said. "I'm not even mad, because you don't look good at all."

Hiked up to the level of the street, I could hear the flow of cars, and the existence of other human beings switched back on as quickly as it had switched off. I felt invisible in the darkness, like the water underneath me. I didn't want to go back to the Egyptian Bar, its light bright against the black sky. I didn't feel like talking to anyone there. Or maybe on the planet.

I followed Vonn back in though, and let her lead me to a stool at the counter.

"I'm buying you a burger," she announced, and nagged the bartender about his grilling technique, but he just grinned and ignored other customers. I stared at myself in the big glass, at the life in the edges of the reflection. The light seemed extra brittle, the jukebox vague, a sound that drew me into half a trance. I didn't know who was real.

The burger and fries started to bring me back to a level of normalcy, like I hadn't felt in months. Vonn was scrutinizing me.

"Where did you go?" she persisted.

"Nowhere. I was there."

"You know there wasn't any fog."

Of course not.

"How much do you weigh?" she asked suddenly. I just shook my head.

"Not much, but that's beside the point."

"So what happened?"

"I was talking to a ghost. It was just for a minute, but it feels like we talked for hours." Just saying it, something recognizable as me settled back down into chest, my limbs, my body waking up. "I told you about the creepy guy in the basement? Now I feel bad that I thought he was so creepy. He's just dead. He's been dead as long as I've known him. There's ghosts everywhere, in this bar, right now."

She didn't laugh, but spun a little in the stool, scanning around the room. "That doesn't seem implausible."

"We can't see gravity." I shook my empty plastic burger basket. "We can't see taste."

"Fuck. We can't even see music."

She looked at me for a second and said, "Get your beer. Let's go find James."

41.

"But the symbols
Of the Invisible are the loveliest
Of what is visible ..."
— George Gordon, Lord Byron, *Cain*

42.

The rest of the summer went on the same way. We met at the Egyptian Bar, where we had stupid conversations that made me laugh, and I drank beer that was lying around. Sometimes, through the din on a busy Saturday, when I was starting to think I'd dreamed it, I'd glimpse the old-timer in the seed cap, leaning at the bar, talking to a biker dude, but only from a distance. Even Data Entry Hell came to an end. I saved enough for fall semester, and the campus began to bristle again with purpose. I couldn't write off my life yet.

Dr. Bleak's channel started to lose its signal and had all but disappeared, and I knew I was going to have to start being the horror host for my own life. Some weekends after barclose, when I tried to tune in, I found a shadowy puppet show of actors fuzzy on the screen, but I couldn't make out anything they said. He disintegrated into static. I thought, someday, when I'm the professor from an old movie who's an expert on the occult, I'll write a book about him. That was all I could do, and maybe he'd hear about it, wherever he was, where spirits go after they fade away.

About the author

Karen Joan Kohoutek has published four previous books through Skull and Book Press: *The Jack-o-Lantern Box*, a novella about a small-town Halloween; the poetry book *Votive: Poems and Oracle*; *Ici Repose: A Guide to St. Louis Cemetery No. 2, Square 3*, which is a detailed reference guide to the New Orleans cemetery; and *Mrs. Crowe's Christmas Ghosts*, a version of Catherine Crowe's 1859 collection of "friend of a friend" supernatural tales. She publishes nonfiction, mostly on pulp fiction and cult films, for a variety of websites print publications, and essay collections, including two books in the Blackwell Philosophy and Pop Culture Series. She lives in Fargo, North Dakota, where she tries not to miss *Svengoolie* and *The Last Drive-In*.